# LITTLE
# VIKING HORSE

## CATHERINE HOLLAND-BAX

Text copyright Catherine Holland 2021

First Published in Great Britain by EponaWise Limited
Email: contact@eponawise.com
www.eponawise.com

Cover and interior design by Alison Withey
Cover images by Nicola Guenigault
Illustrations and Gait Map by Mic Rushen, Solva Icelandics

Little Viking Horse* is a registered trade mark in the UK

ISBN: 978-1-9196301-0-6

Little Viking Horse is a work of fiction and all characters are a product
of the author's imagination, with the exception of some of the horses
who do actually exist! Events in the story are also fictional, though many
are based on real experiences, and observations made by the author.

Dedicated to the memory of
**Roger Alan Bax**
1960 - 2016

My husband and soulmate
A proud nurse and humble horseman

# LITTLE VIKING HORSE'S GAITS

A gait is a pattern of steps or way of walking

There is more information on the gaits and
Icelandic horses in the back of the book

## CHAPTER 1
### A Wobbly Beginning

A newborn foal, black as lava, dropped steaming into the straw, as a storm battered the wooden walls of the barn, threatening to tear it down. Outside the clouds in the night sky obscured the full moon, but inside a shiny crescent moon was clearly visible on the foal's forehead, and a little white streak like a fork of lightning danced on the end of his nose. The mare turned to lick him, but before he was even dry she began to push him with her nose.

He was less than an hour old and did not yet have his own name, so she just called him her little Viking.

*Come, Little Viking Horse, on your feet.*

At first Little Viking Horse didn't know what to do with his disobedient legs, and each time he tried to stand he just ended up in a heap on the straw again. But his mother kept encouraging him with gentle shoves and kicks, until finally he was standing on all four legs. Wobbling a bit, but he was standing.

## CHAPTER 2
### Horses Don't Get to Choose

Fleygur felt apprehensive about Mr Jones from the moment he saw him striding across the yard, tapping a whip on the side of his long black riding boots. As he watched the man approach Fleygur's eyes widened and his ears stood to attention. A long-legged man with broad shoulders, Jones was smartly dressed in a tweed jacket with a shirt and tie, but his cream coloured jodhpurs bagged around the top of his thighs, and the waistband sat on his hips, as if they struggled to reach down the whole length of his legs. Jones's sharp blue eyes flickered their focus of attention so quickly that Fleygur struggled to work him out.

Jones marched around like he owned the place, but Fleygur could sense tension in the man. He was loud and acted as if he was in charge, but his breathing and the whole aura around him shouted something else to Fleygur. Was it fear? Anger? Whatever it was, it made Fleygur nervous.

"Where's this Sports Horse of yours then?" demanded Jones, tapping his whip faster.

"Potential Sports Horse, potential," said

Philippa. "He's very talented in the special gaits of the Icelandic horse, and has a lot of energy but, as I said on the phone, he's young, and will need bringing on slowly. This is him…," Philippa reached over the fence to ruffle Fleygur's forelock. "He's called is Flay-gur," she said, sounding out his name.

*She knows what she's talking about,* Fleygur thought, as he lipped affectionately at Philippa's hands. *Talented, that's me.*

"I can…," Philippa hesitated, "…recommend a good instructor near you."

"Instructor!" barked Jones, "I am not a beginner!"

"No, no, Mr Jones, I know you're an experienced horseman, I wasn't suggesting…I didn't mean…it's just…the development of the gaits does require specialist knowledge…to make the most of them…if you want to compete in Icelandic Horse Sport…," she trailed off.

Fleygur snorted and bobbed his head nervously. He didn't like the way that Jones somehow made Philippa look smaller and sound quieter. Fleygur trusted Philippa, she was kind. But she was wary of Jones and that made Fleygur anxious. He shifted his weight from one foot to the other.

*Jones is like an unexploded volcano,* he thought. Fleygur had never seen a volcano, but his best friend Gydja had told him about one erupting in Iceland when she was a foal, suddenly exploding and spitting fire into the sky, sending the horses skittering down the valley to safety.

*This man is like that,* Fleygur thought, *unpredictable.* He quietly stepped back from the fence and turned to put some distance between himself and Jones.

"Whoa, Fleygur," said Philippa. Fleygur stopped and looked back at her as she walked up and quietly popped a halter over his ears, slipping him a nice crunchy treat in the process. "Come on," she said, "Let's show Mr Jones what you can do."

Six months earlier Philippa had sat on Fleygur for the first time, gently teaching him to be a good riding horse, like his mum. He had felt really pleased with himself and let out an excited whicker to Gydja, *look at me, I am a proper riding horse now!*

*I think you will find there is a bit more to it than that,* Gydja had nickered back. *You haven't even got out of walk yet!*

Gydja was wise and kind, and she'd been there ever since Fleygur had been born. When the bigger foals played rough, she would wave her nose to drive them off.

But today Gydja was grazing with the rest of the herd in a paddock nearby, and Fleygur was all grown up and had to look out for himself.

When he was tacked up, and Philippa had checked that everything was comfortable for him, she led him to over to Jones.

In the school Jones mounted and Fleygur set off in walk. It felt strange to have a different rider on his back. Jones was much heavier than Philippa, and just a bit wobbly.

"So, one of the extra gaits is called 'tölt,'" said Philippa. "Sit deep and use your lower leg to ask for more impulsion."

Fleygur tried to organise his legs in just the way he was supposed to, making an even four-beat on the ground. Lifting his front legs high he looked like he was walking very fast with his back legs and trotting at the front. Fleygur considered it strange that humans thought Icelandic horses had only five gaits. He wondered why all his other gaits were not required, such as the tölty-trot, or the tölt with the back legs and canter with the front ones, or his personal favourite, the jiggy-joggy walk, especially useful for when he was in a bit of a hurry but didn't fancy canter.

*Those are not comfortable for your rider*, Gydja had told him. *If you want to be a good riding horse*, she had said, *you have to learn to do the nice even gaits that the humans want*.

"Good," Philippa was saying, "he should tuck his back end under and push with his hind legs…

yes...good, ease up on his mouth a little, he can carry himself...yes, yes...that's it, you've got it!"

*I've got it!* Fleygur thought, *but I wish he wouldn't pull on my mouth, and wiggle in the saddle.*

Gradually his rider became more balanced, and Fleygur could tell that Jones had one of those wrinkly faces, the one that meant humans were happy.

"This tölting is great," said Jones. "Just like gliding along."

"It is," said Philippa, who was smiling now. "He's a good competition prospect...with the right training," she added firmly.

Fleygur was enjoying showing off his tölt, and now Jones was talking to Philippa he was fussing less with his hands and legs. Philippa seemed more relaxed too, talking to Jones about training regimes for Icelandic Horse Sport.

*Maybe Jones will be a good rider after all*, Fleygur thought, *and he wants to take me to competitions. I won't be just a riding horse, I'll be a sport horse too!*

Philippa called to Marcy, the young girl who helped out at weekends. She waited with Fleygur, watching Philippa talking with Jones as they walked toward his car. After a while they shook hands and Jones drove away. Fleygur could feel that Marcy was upset-angry. Humans were complicated and it was hard to know what they were thinking. Sometimes they seemed angry, and then they cried.

As Philippa walked over to join them Marcy kept her gaze lowered, her face partly hidden under her long dark hair.

"What's up?" asked Philippa.

"How you can sell Fleygur to that horrible man?" Marcy said.

Philippa sighed. "You know, you shouldn't always judge people by the gossip you hear. Mr Jones hasn't been around Icelandic horses that long. I know he can be a bit abrasive, but I'm sure he'll be fine, with a few lessons and a bit of help."

Marcy said nothing, keeping her face towards Fleygur as she pulled the bridle over his ears. Fleygur held onto the bit for a moment before letting it drop. He stretched his jaws wide, showing all his teeth in a huge yawn. Marcy tickled the end of his wrinkled nose with the tips of her fingers, and slipped on his halter.

"But Fleygur's sensitive," she said, "he needs gentle handling."

"You're fifteen, Marcy," said Philippa. "Old enough to understand that this is a business. I breed horses, train them and sell them. You're going to have to get used to it, if you want to work in the horse business."

"But—" Marcy protested.

"Marcy!" Philippa snapped. Fleygur jerked his head up in surprise at Philippa's sharp tone.

"I haven't sold a horse since Blossi. I have to live on something! I put a lot of work into the-se horses. It's not easy letting them go. Please! Don't make this harder for me than it already is." She reached out and scratched Fleygur behind his sweaty ears.

Fleygur remembered his friend Blossi leaving, just after he'd had started his training. Blossi hadn't wanted to go into the stable-on-wheels, and by the time Philippa had coaxed him in, Fleygur and the other young horses had gathered around the gate. They whinnied to him as he was driven away, and he shouted back, but there was nothing they could do to stop him being taken away.

"You'll be fine, fella. Won't you?" Philippa said, taking Fleygur's rope from Marcy, and leading him over to the field-gate.

Fleygur hoped so.

*Why don't we get to choose our humans?* Fleygur asked his mum, as they grazed under the trees that evening.

*It just doesn't work that way my Little Viking,* she told him, *but if you are very lucky, you will find the human that is perfectly matched to you. You will know what your rider wants you to do, almost before they ask, and they will understand you, as if they can horse-talk.*

14

*But I want to stay with you,* Fleygur protested, *and little brother Ragnar, and Gydja, and the rest of our herd.*

*I will miss you,* said his mum, *when you go to a new home, but you have to make your own way. That is how it is for us horses. We don't get to choose.*

## CHAPTER 3
### Fleygur's New Home

A few days later, just as Philippa was leading Fleygur in from the field, Jones's car and trailer came rattling into the yard.

"Oh, you're early," Philippa said, with just a trace of annoyance in her voice, though Fleygur was sure Jones didn't notice it. "I was just going to get him ready for you, and make sure he's calm and settled."

"No need," barked Jones, "I've a business meeting to get to. Just load him up and I'll be on my way."

"Okay," said Philippa, frowning.

Fleygur felt jumpy, he didn't like it when humans were snappy, even if they weren't snapping at him. It wasn't a great start to his new life, with Jones saying, "Yes... Yes...," impatiently as Philippa tried to give last minute advice on settling a new horse. She led Fleygur straight on to the trailer, muddy coat and all, and gave him a quick scratch behind the ear.

"Be good," she whispered.

Before Fleygur had a chance to call out to

his field-mates the ramp was closed. He heard Ragnar's high pitched foal-whinny calling to him, and Fleygur nickered anxiously as the trailer bounced and rattled out through the gateway. He had to quickly sidestep to keep balanced as they turned onto the road. He craned his neck around to look behind and could just see Philippa standing in the middle of the lane, watching them go. Now *he* was leaving! On his own, without his mum, his herd, without Gydja! He started to panic and tugged at the rope that tied him to the front of the trailer. He stamped his foot on the floor and whinnied as loud as he could, *I'm here, I'm here...where are you?*

*Good-bye Little One,* came Gydja's whinny from the field.

*Gydja, help me!* Fleygur called back, his neck stretched rigid, nose pointed forward to get maximum volume, *Gydja, Gydja!* But this time there was no reply. His heart pounded in his chest, his ears flicked in all directions as he tried to make sense of the cacophony of noise surrounding him. He stamped again, his hooves thumping on the echoey floor. Bang, bang, bang. Suddenly the trailer stopped dead, and Fleygur stumbled forward against the breast bar. Shocked, Fleygur planted all four feet firmly and braced himself, waiting for the next violent lurch of the floor. He could just hear Jones's voice, muffled though the wall of the trailer, "Cut it out!" he growled.

They pulled off again but just as Fleygur was getting used to the movement, the trailer slowed sharply and Fleygur was jolted forward again. His eyes widened in surprise. He was just repositioning his feet when the trailer lurched over to one side and Fleygur was slammed against the side wall, and then, a moment later, he was thrown the other way. He spread his legs apart and leaned back on the rear bar to try to stay on his feet.

All was well for a while and then...bang, he was thrown forward again. His whole body tensed with anticipation, and his muscles trembled with the effort. Sweat trickled down his chest and between his front legs, making streaks in the mud on his coat, before it dripped onto the floor. He'd travelled in a stable-on-wheels before but it had been smooth and calm. Now it was like Jones had forgotten he was there at all, being bounced around behind the car.

Eventually the route became smoother and the trailer stopped lurching about. Fleygur's muscles relaxed and he swayed gently from side to side as they sped down the motorway. He could hear the roar of engines as they passed the lorries in front of them. His eyelids drooped as he dozed, letting the noise of the engines, and the rattles of the trailer drift away.

Finally the motion stopped all together, and the engine went quiet. Fleygur heard muffled voices outside the trailer, and he pawed the ground with one hoof. *Get me out of here,* he thought. His ears flickered rapidly as he heard the sound of bolts being drawn back, then the front ramp lowered.

"Well, you're in a bit of a state," said Jones, untying him and leading him from the trailer. "Let's get you hosed down."

All Fleygur really wanted to do was have a good roll and get some grass inside of him. He needed food, and urgently! But he stood patiently, while Jones washed him and inspected his legs.

"Well, no damage there. We're going to be doing a lot of travelling, so you'd best get used to this," he said, and gave Fleygur a hearty slap on the neck. Fleygur jerked his head up in alarm, but Jones was grinning at him with one of those wrinkly faces, so it seemed that Jones thought this was a sign of affection. Fleygur would have much preferred a nice scratch on his shoulder, or behind his sweaty ears, like Philippa used to do.

Jones led Fleygur from the yard and past a small stone building with an iron railing fence. Two huge brown and black dogs bounced up and down at the railings, barking and wagging their tails furiously. Fleygur eyed them warily and stretched his nose down to get a proper sniff of them.

"Shut it!" Jones snapped at the dogs. Instantly their tails dropped and they slunk back to their kennel, whining. Jones led Fleygur into a huge field with lots of separate paddocks, already occupied by other horses. Fleygur lifted his nose and whinnied, *Hello, it's me!*

The horses' heads lifted from their grazing, ears swivelled in Fleygur's direction. The noses of some horses vibrated as they nickered a greeting, and two of them followed Fleygur along the line of the fence, their heads and ears tipped forward in curiosity.

*I'm Jinks,* said a dapple grey horse, *are you my replacement?*

*I am here to train for competitions,* said Fleygur.

Jinks seemed satisfied with that answer, and maybe even a bit relieved. *This is Lina,* said Jinks, waving his nose at the sandy coloured mare next to him. *She's a New Forest pony, and she's MY friend.*

*Do you mind!* snorted Lina, putting her ears back as Jinks got too close, *I will be friends with whomever I choose,* and just to make sure that Jinks got the message, she gave him a good hard nip on the top of his leg. Jinks skipped sideways, out of reach before she could bite him a second time.

Fleygur was excited to meet new horses, but when he reached out to sniff noses with Jinks and Lina, Jones held his rope tight and he couldn't reach them.

"I've prepared a nice paddock of your own where you can say hello to this lot without any of you silly buggers getting kicked," Jones said, pulling Fleygur's head away from his new friends. "Can't be having my new competition horse injured before we start now can we?"

Two really big horses watched as Fleygur was turned out into a paddock between them and Jinks and Lina. He wondered if they'd be friendly, but top of his mind was that longed-for roll, and as soon as Jones slipped off the halter he dropped down to the ground.

"Not there you silly idio…," but Jones's warning was already too late, as Fleygur's leg caught in the electric fence and ZAP! He scrambled to his feet and tried to run from whatever it was that had just bitten him, but the tape caught around his back legs, and as he ran the poles were ripped from the earth and chased after him, bouncing and leaping and pulling on the tape, as they first snagged in the ground, and then tore free again. Fleygur put his head down and ran faster, but now the posts were not all that was chasing him! In hot pursuit were the two big horses. The first, a huge black cob with a white blaze on his face, and following him, an equally huge red mare, whose mane streamed out behind her like dancing flames. Round and round the field he ran with the two big horses behind him, bucking in excitement. Every so often Fleygur caught sight of Jones flapping his arms and waving a halter around. He thought maybe he could hear Jones shouting "Whoa... whoa...." But he was too busy running for his life to be sure.

## CHAPTER 4
### Roger

When the biting fence had finally come free from his legs, and the poles had stopped chasing him, he became aware of another human voice in the field. A gentler younger voice.

"Easy, boy," he called. "I'll get him, Mr Jones. He's scared is all."

"Stupid more like," said Jones lobbing a halter to the boy. "Fine, you sort him out. I've got things to do. He's made me late already…and Roger…"

"Yes Mr Jones?"

"None of that horse whispering, hugging nonsense. He's a horse not a teddy bear! Catch him, put him back and get on with your chores. I pay you to sweep the yard and shovel crap. Not all that communing-with-nature rubbish."

"Yes Mr Jones," the boy said, keeping a steady gaze on Fleygur. Fleygur stood watching the boy, his sides heaving as his breathing slowly returned to normal.

The boy had a mop of sandy blond hair and blue eyes. Not sharp and piercing like Jones's, but silvery-blue like a clear winter sky. He was not as big as Marcy, and looked very small compared to the looming figure of Jones, who was now striding back towards the yard. Fleygur watched cautiously as the boy stepped between him and the other two horses, his nostrils widening as he breathed in the boy's scent. The boy made a low murmuring noise and stepped a little closer, reaching out to touch the side of Fleygur's head. Fleygur felt no need to move, the presence of the boy calmed him. Running his hand down Fleygur's neck the boy slipped his arm around him, and held him in a hug. It felt strange, but Fleygur didn't feel trapped. Somehow feeling the boy's heart beating as he pressed against him made Fleygur feel safe. He stayed absolutely still as the boy slid the halter up over his nose and buckled it in place. Then the boy just stood with him a while. No pressure, just standing, and breathing.

There was something about this boy, who demanded nothing in that moment. Fleygur's breathing slowed, and after a few minutes it was as if they were breathing as one. This was a boy he could trust, this boy, Roger. Fleygur felt sure of it.

The two big horses seemed very happy with their afternoon antics and were still play-fighting as Roger led Fleygur back to his paddock. When Roger slipped the halter off Fleygur was reluctant to leave him. He nuzzled at the boy's hands, his eyes large and soft and his breathing calm. Roger smiled and rubbed his forehead.

"Nice little fella aren't you?" Roger said, stepping back and eyeing him up and down. "Strong too, by the looks of it. Bet you're clever as well. Look at you with those big brown eyes." Roger's gaze drifted off for a moment, and a small smile played around his lips. "I wish you could be my...," he began, but then he gave a little shake of his head, and scratching Fleygur behind his ears, he turned and headed back to the yard.

Fleygur followed the boy for few steps. He wanted to stay with this small quiet human, but his belly informed him it was time to eat, and as the boy disappeared into the barn Fleygur dropped his head to graze. After filling his empty stomach with some nice tasty grass, and with his newly found respect for the fence that bites, he trotted over to say a proper hello to the other horses.

Fleygur had not seen really big horses before, not close up. At Philippa's farm, where he had been born, they were all Icelandic horses, and none were as huge as these. He nickered a soft greeting.

The big black horse snorted and looked down his long broad nose at Fleygur, *who are you?*

*I'm Little Viking Horse. The humans call me*

*Fleygur, it means 'flying one,'* replied Fleygur proudly. *I'm an Icelandic horse,* he said, showing off his tölt and tossing his mane. *We're special horses, horses of the Vikings!*

*A HORSE?* the red mare snorted. *You are not a horse. Much too small! Are you sure you are not a Shetland pony? Or a Donkey!* And she trotted away across the field with the black horse following, tossing his head.

Fleygur wasn't at all sure he liked being called a pony, not that he minded Shetland ponies, or donkeys, or big horses come to that, as long as they were not as rude as the two he had just met. So, he was a small horse. He didn't mind. He knew he was an Icelandic horse, the strong, fast and noble horse of warriors. His mum had told him so. He could do an awesome tölt too, and he could do the super fast 'flying pace.' That's how he got his human-given name. Philippa had seen him in the paddock one day, racing with his friends, Blossi and Thor, and he had shot past them all in flying pace and earned his name.

*Blossi?* Suddenly he missed his friends. *Where was Gydia? And Ragnar, and his mum...,* Fleygur jerked his head up and scanned the field, his heart pumping hard. He called out, a half hopeful whinny, but they must have been too far away to hear him. He wondered if he would ever see any of them again.

A few days later Jones took down the electric fencing and allowed Fleygur in with the other horses. The big black horse who chased him the first day was grazing in the middle of the field. *He's really huge,* thought Fleygur.

*Who's the big fat Cob?* he asked Lina.

*Don't let him hear you calling him that!* said Lina. *His name is Beanie, and he's the boss-horse. Don't mess with him. And that red mare, she's Ginger. Best stay out of her way. She's a Polo Pony, used to getting her own way.*

Fleygur pricked his ears in Beanie's direction. *He's big, but he doesn't seem mean,* he thought, *I just need to let him think he's the boss.*

Fleygur pressed his nose up to Jinks's, and breathed for a moment. *Are you a New Forest pony too?* he asked.

*I'm not a pony of any sort! I'm a race horse,* said Jinks. *Jones wanted me to do Cross Country courses, but he said I don't jump big enough. I jump fine once he's fallen off!* Jinks snorted and playfully nipped Fleygur's nose. Fleygur's head shot up in the air and he tossed his mane, then he nipped Jinks in return. Lina stepped smartly out of the way as Jinks and Fleygur gambolled past, biting at each others legs. It felt good to be able to charge about and play-fight with his new herd.

The next morning Jones could be heard barking orders to Roger in the yard, and then, after he'd had him running this way and that for half an hour, he called to the boy,

"Roger, get that horse ready."

"Yes Mr Jones."

Jinks and Lena stopped grazing as the boy approached the field.   Jinks's nostrils tensed. *Jones is going to ride,* he snorted. Fleygur twitched nervously as the trickle of tension passed though the herd.

*So what,* said Fleygur, a little more boldly than he actually felt. *I've done this riding thing before. It's not so hard.*

*You've not met the REAL Jones yet,* snorted Jinks, taking two steps back as Roger approached the little group with a halter in his hand.

"Not you today Jinks, it's Fleygur's turn," he said, slipping the halter over Fleygur's ears. He gave Jinks a little scratch before leading Fleygur away.

"We have to get you fitter," he said to Fleygur. "Jones says you are not muscled up enough yet. I told him you are still young, but he—"

"Stop jabbering to that horse and come on," barked Jones.

"Yes Mr Jones." Roger didn't say any more, but as he got Fleygur ready he gave him lots of reassuring scratches. He brushed the mud from

Fleygur's coat, paying close attention to where his girth would go, picked the mud and stones from Fleygur's feet and put on the saddle. He held the bit up to Fleygur's mouth and Fleygur took it between his teeth as the boy slid the leather bridle over his ears. Fleygur liked this boy. He talked to him with his body and his feeling, even when he was not actually speaking. Horse-talk, the horses called it, and Fleygur's mum had told him that only really sensitive and clever humans could do it. Even then, they were just beginners compared to horses. Every horse wished for a horse-talking human as their owner, and one day Fleygur hoped to have one too.

Roger chuckled as he struggled to get the bridle over Fleygur's huge forelock. Fleygur liked the sound of Roger's laugh, it made him feel relaxed. Roger buckled up the nose band and slipped two fingers between the band and Fleygur's nose.

"Not too tight," he said, and led Fleygur to where Jones was waiting.

Jones looked Fleygur up and down. Then he tightened the nose band. Fleygur's mouth was strapped shut, and his soft lips were pressed uncomfortably against the bit in his mouth. Jones glared at the boy. Roger quickly lowered his eyes. Neither of them spoke, but it seemed to Fleygur that a lot was being said.

As Jones swung up into the saddle his toes

jabbed into Fleygur's ribs and Fleygur jumped forward in surprise. He got a sharp jab in the mouth in return as Jones yanked on the reins. Fleygur stopped dead and chewed nervously on the bit. He was starting to feel confused about what Jones wanted him to do. He had to keep shifting his feet to stay balanced as Jones lurched around in the saddle, pointing out a long list of jobs for Roger to do while they were out.

"Right," said Jones, after he'd finished issuing orders. "Let's see if we can get some fire in this horse's belly."

# CHAPTER 5
## A Spirited Horse

Jones gave Fleygur a sharp kick in the ribs with his heels, sending him clattering out of the yard in tölt. Jones seemed happy that they were moving so fast, and was urging him on, so Fleygur kept running. Fleygur could do fast, fast was good. Fast was the best way to escape scary things and pain, and the best way to get home to your friends as quickly as possible.

When they reached the end of the long drive they turned onto a narrow lane with neatly trimmed hedges and Jones allowed him to walk for a while, letting the reins go long. Fleygur gratefully lowered his head, stretching his neck muscles, but before he had fully regained his breath they turned onto another bridleway and Jones kicked him back into fast tölt. Although he didn't know exactly where he was Fleygur knew instinctively that they had turned back towards his new herd, and he wanted to get back to them as fast as he could. The faster they went the more Jones pushed his feet forwards in the stirrups and leant back, pushing the saddle uncomfortably into Fleygur's loins.

Sweat started to trickle down Fleygur's legs. His nostrils were wide and stiff, like great big pipes, as he tried to suck in as much oxygen as he could to feed his tiring muscles. The pressure of the saddle was really hurting his back.

*The quicker I get home,* he thought, *the sooner I can have this saddle off.*

His mane flew about wildly as they sped down the bridleway. The rutted muddy path had been baked hard by the sun and Fleygur's feet were moving so quickly that he struggled to keep an even tempo. Then, he tripped, and as he stumbled down onto his knees, Jones landed heavily on Fleygur's neck, grabbing handfuls of his mane. Fleygur's nose grazed the ground before he managed to stagger back to his feet. Jones was still on board, but no longer holding the reins. Finding his reins loose, and nothing to hold him back, there was barely a pause before Fleygur set off again in his mad dash for home, with Jones bouncing around in the saddle, grunting and cursing.

When Jones finally managed to pick up the reins again Fleygur felt the unforgiving metal press hard onto the soft part of his jaw. He tried to open his mouth to ease the pain, but the nose-band was fastened tight and pinched his face. Struggling for some relief, he stuck his nose up in the air and gripped the bit between his teeth. It was hard to run like this with the saddle pressing harder on his sore back. He was sweating, and his muscles felt like they were burning, but even though Jones kept pulling the reins Fleygur was sure that getting home was the most important thing. Everything else was blocked from his mind as they raced up the long drive.

They arrived back home at full fast tölt, almost skidding into an open-mouthed Roger, who was standing in the middle of the yard.

"Now, that's what I call a spirited horse!" said Jones leaping from the saddle and throwing the reins to the boy, before striding off. Fleygur was exhausted. He dropped his head, his nostrils wide and his sides heaving.

Roger was very quiet when he removed Fleygur's bridle and saddle, and sponged the sweat from Fleygur's neck and chest. The boy's jaw was tight and his lips a thin line. His eyes looked blurry and wet. Fleygur sensed a bubbling anger, but he knew it was not aimed at him. Roger's movements remained gentle as he carefully washed Fleygur's legs and checked his legs and feet. Then he fished a little red nobbly bar from his pocket and held it up for Fleygur to smell. The rubber was wiffy and Fleygur puckered up his top lip, pointing his nose into the air to get a good sniff of the strange new smell that mingled with the scent of the boy. Roger laughed and started to massage Fleygur's shoulders and back with the rubber bar. It felt very good, and Fleygur lowered his head, his eyes drooping as his sore muscles began to unknot. Finally, Roger gave Fleygur's forehead a little rub, and sighed.

"Sorry boy. Jones is not always quite as crazy as that," he said.

Fleygur gladly followed Roger back to the field, where the rest of the herd were crowded around the gate. Roger shooed them all back and led Fleygur through. Fleygur dropped straight down for a roll to ease his muscles, and as he got up Jinks reached out to try and nip Fleygur into playing.

*Get off*, Fleygur said, waving his nose and putting his ears back at his friend.

Jinks waved his nose around too, trying to playfully bite Fleygur's neck, *I missed you* he said, *let's play*.

*Enough running, I want to eat*, Fleygur said, as they bobbed their heads around each other in a phoney fight. They stopped, with ears pricked, when they spotted Roger crossing the yard with a wheel-barrow piled high with hay. Fleygur nickered, excited by the sweet smell as Roger threw the hay over the fence, one pile for each of them, Beanie tried to drive the others away with flat-ears, but eventually they all settled to eat, with Roger watching from the gate. Fleygur happily munched on his hay, feeling the calmness spreading though the herd.

*He's a good colt, that Roger,* said Beanie, raising his head as he chewed. *Sensible head for one so young. Some humans never get as much sense as that one.*

*Is he young?* asked Fleygur.

*He's like a three year old colt,* said Lina, *maybe ten or eleven in human years. Humans are slow developers,* she said knowingly.

Ginger and Jinks agreed that the boy was a good example of the human species, and Jones was definitely not. Lina said that she was very lucky that she was not actually Jones's pony, her woman just paid for her to live here, so Jones had never ridden her. Fleygur twitched his ears as he ate, and listened. The hay was good, but something about the talk of Jones made him edgy.

Fleygur snuffled up every last strand of his share of the hay, and gingerly stepped closer to Beanie's pile. Beanie flattened his ears again and Fleygur retreated a step, but he wasn't giving up that easily. Keeping a careful eye on the big horse's ears, he edged his way closer again, stopping if Beanie's ears twitched in his direction. When he was as close as he dared, he reached out with one hoof and dragged some straggly bits of hay towards him, until he could wrap his lips around it, the long strands of hay pulling other bits with it.

"Ha!" shouted Roger from the gate. "Like eating spaghetti! Clever little horse!"

Two days later Jones was back in the yard, and this time Fleygur wasn't so keen to come in from the field. He planted his feet firmly.

"Come on," said Roger, giving a little pull on the halter. "Walk-on." But Fleygur still felt anxious being away from his familiar home and herd, and now he was making new friends he didn't want to risk leaving them, in case they disappeared too! He leant back against the rope. Roger frowned.

"What's up?" Roger said, stepping forward and giving Fleygur's forehead a little rub. If it was just the boy he'd have been quite happy to go in and be tacked up, but he could see Jones pacing around the yard and tapping his whip on his boots. Fleygur flinched at the tap-tap-tap.

"COME ON BOY!" yelled Jones from the yard. "Get that horse in here."

"Yes Mr Jones...Come on Fleygur, pleeease! You'll get me into trouble," said Roger, giving a little tug on the rope. Fleygur switched his attention back to the boy and followed him into the yard.

"I've marked out an Oval Track in the winter

field," Jones said to Roger, as he was tacking Fleygur up. "It's what we compete on in Icelandic Horse Sport," he said.

The boy looked a little surprised that Jones was actually speaking to him in a normal voice, rather than barking orders, and just made a 'mm' noise in response. Jones continued, "There's a show shortly in the New Forest, then I've entered one in Germany next month, and in September there's the Icelandic Horse British Championships. This horse and I are going to take the competition scene by storm!" Jones announced, as he strode off to get his riding hat.

Roger whispered into Fleygur's ear, "British Championships, Fleygur! I bet you're good enough too, shame that Jones has no more idea about what he's doing than I would! Wish it could be me that rode you. We could do it, couldn't we?" Roger tickled Fleygur's nose and Fleygur licked the boy's palm, enjoying the faint taste of the treats he knew were tucked in the boy's pocket for later.

Roger had been right about Jones, though. After that first crazy ride he did seem to calm down a little. They didn't spend the whole time careering around in a fast tölt, instead they spent a lot of time going round the Oval Track, practicing the different gaits. But once a week Jones would take him for what he called 'a blast,' and they would be back to fast tölting along the lanes. His back always felt sore, but with the adrenaline pumping round his veins, he gripped the bit between his teeth and ran. Mostly he was so focused on running that he didn't even notice when Jones pulled harder on the reins. As far as he was concerned, when Jones tensed up and pulled, that meant run, and run fast.

## CHAPTER 6
### A Lesson from Philippa

One morning Fleygur heard a familiar engine
sound coming up the long drive. A bubble of
excitement rippled through him, and he let out a
quiet nicker of recognition.

*What is it?* Ginger asked, lifting her head from
grazing.

*The Woman!* Fleygur nickered, setting off at a
brisk trot towards the gate, and sliding to a halt
just as Philippa got out of her car.

"Well, hello Fleygur," she said with a broad
grin on her face. "What have you been up to?"

Fleygur had no idea what she meant, but it
was good to smell her familiar scent. He snuffle-
snorted her hands and frisked her pockets for
treats. She ruffled his mane and looked around
the yard. Spotting Roger leaning on a broom,
quietly watching them, she walked over.

"Hi, Philippa Marshall, I'm here for the
lesson, can you let Mr Jones know?"

"Sure," said Roger turning to go, but then he
paused, and turned back. "He likes you, Fleygur
does," he said quickly.

"He's one of mine, bred and trained him myself," said Philippa looking back at Fleygur and smiling. Fleygur bobbed his head at the sound of her voice. He liked it when she talked, especially when she was saying nice things about him.

"He's a lovely sensitive horse. It's good to see him again. Mr Jones said he was having a few issues with him, so I have come to see if I can help. All part of the service," she said turning back to Roger.

"Nothing wrong with the *horse*," mumbled Roger as he turned towards the house.

*Smart boy,* thought Fleygur, *nothing wrong with me at all!*

Philippa watched Roger go, but when she turned back to Fleygur, her face was wrinkled with concern.

"Everything okay?" she asked him, giving him a scratch.

Fleygur wished he could tell her it was not. He nuzzled at her hands. He wished he could tell her that his back was sore, and that he had a pain in his mouth. He wished he could tell her that Jones's riding confused him, and that it hurt his mouth when Jones pulled so hard, but he could not. So he just licked her hands and stood quietly with her, waiting.

The moment was broken by the 'tap-tap-tap' of Jones's whip on his long black boots. Fleygur twitched his ears and stepped back to turn away. Philippa glanced at him with a frown, and then turned and strode over to Jones with her hand outstretched, "Good Morning Mr Jones."

Roger wandered over and stood with Fleygur, running his fingers down his neck and digging his finger nails into Fleygur's favourite itchy spot between his front legs. Despite the nearness of Jones, and the growing tension prickling the air, Fleygur stretched his nose forward, and puckered up his lips in appreciation. Roger put his free hand up to Fleygur's mouth, and Fleygur lipped at his palm.

"No teeth!" said the boy softly. It wasn't necessary. Mutual grooming was very relaxing, but humans were delicate things, and Fleygur knew that teeth were strictly for other horses.

"Get that horse ready," Jones shouted across to Roger.

"Um, I think it might be an idea if you did that yourself," said Philippa, "It'll give me an idea of how you're getting on as a partnership."

Jones shot her an angry look, and Fleygur thought he might be about to shout, but instead he marched over and snatched the halter from the gatepost. Fleygur stood very still while he was haltered, as he knew he was expected to, but he anxiously swished his tail as Jones led him to the yard.

"Get on with your chores then," Jones snapped at Roger, who quickly lowered his eyes and moved away. Philippa's frown lines deepened. Fleygur wanted to follow Roger, but he didn't dare move. As Jones threw the saddle over Fleygur's back, the heavy metal stirrups banged into his sides. Still he didn't move, but Philippa's mouth was drawn into a tight line. Roger, making a half-hearted attempt at sweeping the yard, looked between Fleygur and Philippa. Roger understood how Fleygur felt, Fleygur was sure he did, and maybe Philippa was beginning to get it too. Fleygur turned his head away slightly as Jones held up the bridle, his small silent protest at what he thought was about to follow, but as usual Jones seemed to have no idea what Fleygur was trying to say. Jones grabbed his nostrils hard and yanked his head around.

"Um, Mr ...," started Philippa, but before she could intervene Jones banged the bit against Fleygur's front teeth, and shoved roughly until Fleygur opened his mouth. The bit sat against the growing sore spot on his jaw, and Fleygur clamped his teeth to try and hold the bit still. Jones swung into the saddle, landing heavily. He pulled Fleygur around with the reins and faced him towards the school. Philippa followed at a slow walk, Roger shuffling a short distance behind, still pretending to brush the yard, as he edged closer to the school. Fleygur was glad that the boy was there, it made him feel a little better.

The lesson started badly, with Jones leaning back, pulling on the reins and booting Fleygur in the sides with his heels. Fleygur stuck his nose in the air and braced himself against the pain in his mouth and back, as he tölted around the school. It wasn't a nice even four-beat, as it was supposed to be. Fleygur was having trouble keeping his balance with Jones pulling on him so much.

*I could do better on my own,* thought Fleygur. *Some humans wouldn't have horses, not if the horses got to choose.*

After a few minutes Philippa called out, "Right, Mr Jones, I think I get the picture. Let's give him a break now."

"He's hardly done anything! He's not even broken a sweat," said Jones, but he dropped the reins, and Fleygur gratefully lowered his head towards the ground, stretching the huge muscle on the top of his neck. He rested one foot to ease the pressure on his back. Every minute or so he shifted his weight to the other foot, as Jones and Philippa talked.

"See, the damn horse won't stand still," said Jones after a few minutes, giving a yank on the reins. Fleygur shook his head in protest.

"Why don't you hop off for a while," said Philippa "We can talk through some basics that

I think might help."

Fleygur snorted a sigh of relief as Jones dismounted. He could see Roger leaning on the railings, carefully watching everything Philippa did, as she moved Fleygur's saddle forward and loosened his nose band, all the time talking to Jones about 'setting up the right feel,' and 'building a relationship' with the horse. Jones's face looked as if he had eaten something bitter. His right eye was twitching and he looked like he was about to explode. But Jones just got back on without a word. Fleygur swished his tail as he felt Jones's tension humming through his body, but Jones remained silent, and as he followed Philippa's instructions, the humming slowly reduced.

Fleygur was sure however, that he could still feel the volcano, bubbling deep down inside.

By the end of the lesson Fleygur was feeling a lot more comfortable. Jones's riding had become a little more gentle, and Philippa and Roger had lost their tight faces. Philippa was even smiling.

"That's nice, Mr Jones. A good relaxed walk with long strides," she said. "Let's leave it there, shall we. It's good to finish on a positive. We can work on more next time."

"Next time! What makes you think there will be a next time?" muttered Jones under his breath, but only Fleygur heard him. Jones silently untacked Fleygur, and he even turned him out into the field himself. Fleygur missed his massage from Roger. He dropped down on the ground for a long roll, and as he stood up for his whole body shake he saw Jones throw the halter at the boy. Roger caught it in both arms and held it to his chest, watching Jones as he grunted a gruff goodbye to Philippa, then leaving her standing in the middle of the yard, Jones walked into the house and slammed the door.

Fleygur was feeling much more relaxed, now the lesson was over, and he always felt a whole lot better once Jones had departed too. Roger hopped over the gate and walked towards him. Fleygur dropped his head low and let out a huge sigh, snorting onto the ground and blowing up little clouds of dust. He kept his head lowered while Roger scratched behind his ears. *This boy always knows where to scratch,* Fleygur thought, and if he didn't Fleygur could soon put him right, by shuffling around until the part of his body he wanted scratching was close to the boy's hands.

"Fleygur likes you too," Philippa said to Roger, who smiled shyly. "I didn't know Mr Jones had a son."

Roger's head snapped up. "He's not my dad!" he said, practically spitting out the words.

Fleygur's head jerked up, surprised at the sudden change of emotion from the boy.

"Oh, I'm sorry," Philippa said, "I just assumed

he was. What with the blond hair and blue eyes."

"I just help out at weekends and after school," Roger said. "I like the horses."

"I can see you do," said Philippa, "and you are good with them too. A natural, I'd say."

"Mum taught me...," said Roger.

Fleygur sensed the boy's energy dip as sadness suddenly flowed through his body.

"...before she died," Roger said quietly, looking down at the floor. His hand dropped away from Fleygur's ears.

"Oh, I am so sorry to hear that," said Philippa. "I can't imagine what that must be like for you." She hesitated, and then went on. "She obviously taught you very well. It's lovely that you shared a passion for horses."

Fleygur nudged Roger's elbow, to prompt him to resume his scratching.

"I'd never seen an Icelandic horse before Fleygur," Roger said, brightening a little, and reaching out to give Fleygur a rub. "He's cool. I'd like a horse just like him one day."

"You'd make a lovely partnership," Philippa replied, smiling at the two of them. "Right, I need to get on the road," she said. "It's a long drive. Hopefully I'll see you again Roger, maybe at an Icelandic Horse Show?"

"Yeah, maybe," but Roger didn't sound too certain.

"Bye then," said Philippa, turning and walking towards her car.

Fleygur, ears fixed firmly in Philippa's direction, watched until the car door closed. Then he gave Roger a gentle shove with his nose, to remind him that he hadn't handed over any treats yet. Humans always seemed to forget these basic things when they were talking.

## CHAPTER 7
### That Whip!

Late one afternoon Jones appeared wearing his tweed jacket, smart black jodhpurs and those shiny long black boots, with a scuffed line on the right boot from constant tapping with the whip. He was quieter than usual, as he was getting Fleygur ready to ride, and less rough, but Fleygur was still nervous and shifted his weight from one foot to the other. Fleygur threw his head up when Jones tried to bridle him. He could hear Jones's breathing quickening, and the rising tension prickled though Fleygur's skin. Jones's efforts were punctuated by occasional huffs and muttering under his breath about 'That Woman!'

Fleygur looked around for Roger's reassurance, but the boy wasn't here.

In the school they started off in walk. Jones allowed Fleygur a long rein but, apprehensive about what was to come, Fleygur couldn't help rushing forward. Usually Jones would have pulled hard on the reins to try to slow him, but instead Fleygur could distinctly hear Jones counting.

"In, One-Two-Three-Four. Out, One-Two-Three-Four…"

As Jones's breathing gradually slowed Fleygur adjusted his steps to match the rhythm, and wondered what magic Philippa had performed on Jones. Then came the signal for tölt. Fleygur leapt forward sticking his nose in the air.

"NO," yelled Jones, suddenly yanking on the reins, "SLOWLY, YOU STUPID ANIMAL!"

Fleygur gripped the bit and shook his head in protest. He didn't understand why Jones was suddenly angry, he was only doing what he had always done. Go fast, it's what Jones wanted, wasn't it? Fleygur pulled against the reins and tried to get his head up again, to where the bit hurt less, but Jones just pulled back harder, and pain shot through Fleygur's jaw as the bit pressed onto the sore spot in his mouth. Fleygur's mouth felt like it was on fire. Confused and in pain he plunged his head down and took off in canter. All he could think about was running away from the pain.

Jones tried to turn him sideways, but even with his nose pulled around to his belly Fleygur still tried to run. When he reached the end of the school he couldn't turn without falling over and was forced to stop. Jones was shouting and holding the right rein tight, keeping Fleygur's neck bent. Fleygur was trapped close to the fence as

Jones raised the whip in his left hand, high above his head and, THWACK, THWACK! Two sharp stings bit into Fleygur's thigh. In panic Fleygur twisted sharply away from the pain and Jones's leg smashed into the fence rails. Jones practically threw himself from the saddle, and grabbing the side of the bridle, he raised the whip.

"Pack it in!" he yelled, red in the face.

The whip cut into the soft velvet skin on Fleygur's nose, and the stinging spread across his face. He reared up in fear, but as his hooves hit the ground again the blows rained down on his face. Jones had grabbed the reins and was yanking his head down and flailing at him with the whip. Fleygur, confused and frightened, threw his head around trying to escape Jones's grasp.

Suddenly, Roger was there, running directly at them shouting, "NO, STOP! STOP!" Roger grabbed at the whip and tried to wrestle it from Jones's hands.

"What are you doing, you stupid boy?" screamed Jones.

"You can't hit him like that!" Roger shouted, holding onto the whip with all his might.

Jones twisted the whip from the boy's hands, and almost lost his balance as it came free. He spun around to face Fleygur again, his arms flailing, his mouth opening and closing silently, as his fury overwhelmed his ability to utter any words.

Trapped in the corner of the school Fleygur's head jerked around at the fight in front of him, the whites of his wild eyes flashing in fear, as Roger bravely danced about in front of Fleygur, jumping up and waving his arms to obstruct Jones's attempts to hit him again.

Jones finally found his voice, but he seemed to have lost all sense of who or where he was.

"Don't you know anything?" he screamed at Roger. "You have to dominate the pony, show him who is boss. He is not your friend! HIT HIM, HIT HIM, HIT HIM!"

Jones's cheeks were bright red, and with spittle flying from his mouth he ranted directly into the face of the boy. "You'll never amount to anything. You useless child! You stupid boy!"

Jones raised the whip above his head towering over Roger. As the boy stood there, pale and shaking, Fleygur felt a rush of blood. Unable to flee he screamed his own challenge at Jones, rearing up and striking out with his hooves, narrowly missing Jones's head. Jones froze in the middle of his tantrum, his arm held aloft poised to strike, looking in shock at Fleygur stamping the ground in front of him.

Abruptly the anger disappeared from Jones's face, and he looked between the horse and the boy in confusion. Then he snapped, "Put that horse away and get out of my sight." And he marched out of the school.

"Easy fella," said Roger, as he approached Fleygur, though the boy was trembling as much as he was. Roger wrapped his arms around Fleygur's neck, as he had done the on that first day when they met. "Thank you," he whispered.

Fleygur snorted and huffed away some of his tension. He could feel the boy's heart pounding.

"The man's a bully," said Roger his voice still shaky. "The biggest bully I have ever met. I wish you didn't have to be his horse. I wish…I wish you were mine."

Fleygur nuzzled the boys hands. He wished the boy was his too.

When Roger took Fleygur back to the field, the other horses were on edge and milling around the gate. Ginger had a wild look in her eye.

"Easy girl," said Roger, stretching a hand out to Ginger as he led Fleygur in, but she skipped out of reach and laid her ears back at him. Roger snatched his hand back and looked shocked. Fleygur felt the boy stiffen and jogged on the spot. Jones's outburst had them all wound up, and Fleygur could feel that Roger was still trembling.

Lina waved her nose at Ginger, snorting. *Calm down Ginger, Jones has gone, it's just the boy and little Fleygur.*

Ginger pranced away across the field, as the rest of the herd jostled with each other for a few minutes more, until finally Beanie nuzzled at Fleygur's withers, welcoming him back to the group.

*That was the REAL Jones*, said Jinks.

Jones stayed away for a few days, and the whole herd were glad. It was good to have time to be just horses, to be a herd, without the confusing demands of humans. Fleygur played 'who's the boss' fighting with Jinks, weaving their heads, snapping their teeth, and then galloping off around the field; and one day, even Beanie joined in the fun, bucking and galloping with them up to the trees at the top of the field.

As they stood together resting in the shade, Fleygur risked inviting Beanie to mutually groom, reaching out and nuzzling the roots of the big horse's mane with his lips. Beanie arched his huge neck and nibbled at Fleygur's mane in return. Fleygur had always known Beanie was a big softy really. All that ears back and head waving was just to make sure he got most of the food!

Fleygur looked for Roger at the gate every morning, but he didn't reappear for over a week. When he did, Roger was very quiet and wary of Jones. Jones acted like nothing out of the ordinary had happened, barking his orders at the boy in just the same way that he had done before the incident with the whip. Fleygur kept a very careful eye on Jones too, and especially his whip, being sure to move the instant it was raised. After a while, even Jones noticed he was a bit jumpy and tucked the whip inside his boot. Fleygur hoped that was where it would stay.

# CHAPTER 8
## Fleygur's First Show

One morning, as Fleygur was dozing nose-to-tail with Beanie and swishing flies from each other's faces, Jones brought the stable-on-wheels into the yard and opened the ramps. Ginger bobbed her head anxiously and flared her nostrils with a sharp snort, *I'm not going in that!* she said, spinning around and trotting defiantly to the other side of the field. Fleygur watched as Jones filled the back of his car with stuff. A bucket, a water carrier, a rug, things to make a biting fence, brushes, Fleygur's saddle. *My saddle!* Fleygur wasn't too keen on getting in the stable-on-wheels either, and kicking up his heels he raced after Ginger, putting in a couple of bucks along the way as Beanie and Jinks joined the retreat.

He thought that he had made it perfectly clear that he wanted nothing to do with Jones's plans, but that didn't seem to deter him as here he came, with Fleygur's halter in hand, marching across the field. Fleygur briefly thought about running away, but he knew that he was expected to stand still and be caught, even when all his instincts told

55

him to run. Besides, humans were very persistent. If you walked away they just kept on chasing you. In the end it was a waste of energy to run, so he just waited as Jones fitted his halter and then led him down to the gate.

When they reached the ramp to the trailer Fleygur's nerves got the better of him. He hesitated and looked across at Roger, who was washing out feed-buckets with a hose. The boy's face was tight, and he looked like he was bursting to say something. Ginger was still cavorting around the field, tossing her head wildly and whinnying, *don't go in little horse, don't go in!*

Fleygur could sense Ginger's fear right across the field. He let out a piercing whinny, *Ginger, help me!* sending her into a bucking frenzy.

"Stop winding each other up!" Jones shouted, giving a sharp pull on the rope, and flapping his free hand. "On you get!"

Fleygur pulled back, startled by Jones's shouting and arm waving.

"Do you want me to load him?" asked Roger, appearing around the side of the trailer.

"Fine!" snapped Jones, as he tossed the rope to the boy, "You do it, I've got to get some stuff from the house."

Fleygur was immediately calmer with Roger there, gently rubbing his forehead.

"Stupid man," Roger grumbled, as he took

up the slack in the rope. "Come on Fleygur, I know you don't like it, but look at all that lovely hay in there!" He jiggled Fleygur's rope gently and made a kissing noise. Fleygur knew this was a signal for step forward, and he trusted the boy, so reluctantly he walked up the ramp and into the trailer. Despite his anxiety he was glad of the haynet tied at the front, and tugged out some strands. Slowly the act of chewing calmed him and, with Roger standing quietly nearby, he began to relax.

"Don't worry Fleygur," Roger said, giving him an affectionate scratch behind his ear, "I'll be seeing you tomorrow, Dad's driving me down to watch you! He complained it was a long way on his day off, but he feels bad about leaving me on my own so much, so he's going to do it anyway."

Fleygur didn't really follow what all these words meant, but he liked the soothing sound of Roger's quiet voice.

Suddenly, the car engine started and Fleygur snorted. Jones's voice called out, "Right, shut him in, I'm off!"

Roger gave Fleygur a final rub on his forehead and hopped out through the human sized door at the front. Fleygur nickered nervously as the rear doors closed and the trailer started forward.

The trip was so long that Fleygur's belly had started to rumble. He had finished the hay long ago, and really wanted some nice cool water to hold in his mouth. They had stopped twice along the way, and each time Fleygur thought he was getting out, but Jones just opened the small access door, looked him up and down and shut it again without a word, a treat, or even a scratch. But when they stopped for the third time, the engine of the car finally fell silent. It seemed an age before the ramp was lowered and Jones stepped inside to untie him. Fleygur thought he would burst if he didn't get out soon, and was jigging on the spot as Jones undid his rope.

A small paddock with a biting fence was waiting for him. Fleygur didn't know what to do first, roll, eat, pee, or say hello to the dozens of other horses that surrounded him, so he snatched a couple of mouthfuls of fresh grass, and peed at the same time. He could hear the zap-zap-zap of the biting fence, so when he dropped down for a roll he made very sure to stay in the middle of the tiny paddock. He'd been bitten by a fence like this before, and he wasn't going to make the same mistake twice.

Standing up and having a whole body shake, he looked around. He was in a huge field filled with horses and humans. The place buzzed with activity. There were lots of little paddocks with biting fences, and each one contained an Icelandic horse. Some horses were eating, some sleeping, and others pacing up and down shouting for a friend who wasn't there. Fleygur whickered softly, maybe his own herd were here too? But only a nearby red horse answered his call.

A few horses were going out for a ride with their humans, others were just coming back, and yet more were going around on a track, like the one Jones had marked out at home. Everywhere he looked there were Icelandic horses, in every colour he had ever seen and more. Fleygur had never seen so many horses in one place before.

*I'm at a Show,* he thought. *Now I am going to be a sports horse.*

As the sun dropped below the trees all of the new arrivals for that day settled down, and the camp began to go quiet. Fleygur would have quite liked to stretch his legs properly after the long journey, but he couldn't do much more than walk in small circles in his small paddock, so he settled on eating the hay that Jones had thrown to him before disappearing into his tent.

For most of the night the only sounds from the camp were the gentle munching of horses eating their hay, and the occasional snort or nicker. Fleygur couldn't greet the others properly, with nose touching or nibbling, but he could feel horses all around him, sense their breathing and smell each of their distinct scents. It was a strange disjointed, separated group of horses that he barely knew, but a group of horses was a herd, and that was always better than being alone. He moved to the edge of his paddock, where he was closer to the red horse and hear his gentle breathing. It made him feel safer. The red horse flicked his ears towards him and his nose vibrated a quiet *hello*.

Fleygur was close to finishing his hay when there was a rumble of a lorry in the gateway. Several horses paused their munching and lifted their heads. A human emerged from the passenger side of cab with a torch, and Fleygur blinked as the light bobbed around and flashed in his face as he walked by.

"There's no space here," the man said quietly to the driver in the cab. "Let's try the other field."

A familiar scent wafted into Fleygur's nostrils. *Gydja?* He lifted his head and looked around, nickering softly, but the smell was gone as quickly as it had come. As the trailer moved away Fleygur returned to his hay. In the distance he could hear a horse being led down a ramp, and the noises of a new camp being set up in the neighbouring field. Fleygur chomped on his hay, dozed a little, and chomped on his hay a little more. When finally the hay ran out there was nothing to do but doze, and listen to the occasional hoot of the resident Tawny Owls, and the sounds of the foxes and badgers going about their night time business.

Early the next morning the bustle started up again.

*Is that for me?* nickered Fleygur, as a pile of hay went by on a pair of human legs.

"Sorry fella," said a voice from behind the hay, "You have to wait for Jones."

Every horse had to wait for their particular human to arrive with their breakfast, but that didn't stop them all nickering to any passing human carrying a feed bucket or pile of hay. Fleygur pawed at the ground, *where was HIS breakfast? Where is Jones?*

Then he heard it. A whinny he knew. He threw up his head, his ears pricked in the direction of the call. There, there it was again. *Is it her? It IS her. My Gydja!*

## CHAPTER 9
### Gydja

Fleygur couldn't see her but he whinnied towards the sound, *Gydja, I'm here, I'm here!*

He spun around in his paddock, then stood stock still and listened again, his ears rigid, his muscles so tensed that he almost stopped breathing.

*Hellooo!* came Gydja's whinnying reply, *I am here, where are you?*

Fleygur's heart beat quickened and he tossed his head from side to side, his front feet coming off the ground in excited little jumps. He wanted to gallop and find her but he was stuck in this little paddock. *Gydja!* He must find her, he drew all the air he could into his lungs and stuck his nose out and bellowed has hard as he could, *I'm here, I'm here, I'm here...*

Suddenly a black boot flew past Fleygur's face, only just missing his nose.

"Shut it Fleygur," growled Jones, emerging from the tent.

Fleygur drew breath and prepared for another bellow, but Jones walked directly at him with his whip raised, "I said SHUT IT!"

Fleygur practically stopped mid breath, letting out a stifled snort instead.

"Lay off him a bit, Tony," said a man leading a jet black horse towards the track, "It's your first show isn't it? He'll settle soon enough."

"Mind your own business," snapped Jones turning his back on the man.

Fleygur paced up and down in his paddock, and was starting to get hot. He continued to listen for Gydja, but he kept his noises to an occasional quiet whicker, wary of Jones, who was now advancing towards him with his halter.

Jones tied Fleygur's rope to a metal link on the back of the trailer to get him ready, but Fleygur just couldn't keep still. He was aware of Jones's presence, but almost all his attention was focussed on Gydja. Fleygur swung his back legs round to try and look towards where he had last heard her, banging into Jones in the process.

"Stand still will you," he growled, giving Fleygur a thump in the ribs.

Fleygur swung back the other way and arched his neck to look behind him. He flicked his ears around, and called a few times, each time getting a slap from Jones, though he barely noticed them.

As more and more horses were being tacked up, and setting off with their humans aboard, Fleygur became more agitated, swinging around and pawing the ground. Now his new friends were leaving him too! Fleygur was still dancing about trying to see where they were all going when Jones tried to put his saddle on. As Fleygur side-stepped it promptly slid right over his back and landed on the grass with a thud. Jones grabbed Fleygur's bridle and yanked his head around.

"STAND STILL!" he yelled right into Fleygur's face.

Fleygur smelt bitter coffee on Jones's breath, and could hear his heart pounding. Jones retrieved the saddle from the ground and swung it onto Fleygur's back. The heavy metal stirrups banged into Fleygur's sides and he flinched, but he didn't dare move. Jones tightened the girth and mounted. Landing in the saddle heavily he practically dragged Fleygur around by hauling on the right rein. He was not a small man and Fleygur almost lost his balance. Jones jabbed him in the ribs with his heels and they were off.

"You've no time for a warm up now Tony," said a woman at the entrance to the schooling area, "You'll have to go straight up to the Oval Track."

Fleygur could see three other horses heading up a path between some trees and was happy to follow them at a brisk trot, but then he caught sight of Gydja in a paddock on the other side of the field. He stopped dead, and Jones lurched forward in the saddle, nearly toppling over Fleygur's head. "What the...?"

*GYDJA!* Fleygur whinnied, spinning towards her and dislodging Jones from the saddle in the process.

"Whoaaa..." Thud!

Fleygur, feeling suddenly lighter, broke into a canter. Dodging several grasping hands he covered the length of the field in no time, and slid to a halt next to Gydja. He pressed his nostrils up against her velvet black nose and blew softly. *Gydja,* he breathed, *You are back!*

*Hello Little One,* Gydja nickered, *though I see you are not so little now. You really must take more care with your human. It's not the done thing to dump them on the ground like that,* she said, as she watched Jones limping towards them.

Someone took hold of Fleygur's reins just as Jones arrived, and held one stirrup as he got back on. Fleygur could feel Jones's tense muscles through the saddle. Jones didn't say a word as he turned Fleygur towards the track. Fleygur tried to turn back to Gydja, but Jones kicked his sides, and when Fleygur refused to step forward he received two sharp thwacks from the whip, stinging his thigh. He jumped forward in surprise and started up the path to the Oval Track. But the thought and smell of Gydja still filled his head, and the need to be with her pulled at his attention. He hesitated, thinking to stop and turn around, but Jones's legs were pressed hard against Fleygur's sides, and he held the reins firmly, growling under his breath. Fleygur felt he was being squeezed down a tunnel he didn't want to be in, so he zigzagged up the path. As he zigged near to a metal funnel on the fence, a voice boomed from it.

"Can we PLEASE have Mr Anthony Jones, riding Fleygur, on the track!"

Fleygur jumped at the sound, and zagged quickly to the other side of the path, and almost managed to turn around. Jones's growling exploded into shouting.

"GET ON WITH YOU!" he yelled, and gave Fleygur another thwack. Suddenly Fleygur's mind was back in the school at home, and he panicked. He reared up onto his hind legs shaking his nose to avoid the stinging blows that he expected to come next. Jones grabbed handfuls of Fleygur's mane to stop himself from sliding off, but when Fleygur's front hooves hit the dirt again a quiet familiar voice spoke to him from the side.

"Easy boy." It was Roger!

"I'll give you a lead," he said reaching out to take a rein. "I'm sorry we're late boy," he whispered to Fleygur. Dad got lost!" Soothed by Roger's voice Fleygur allowed himself to be guided up the path. The other horses were already tölting, and as they passed the gate to the track he joined them. Being part of a herd going somewhere was always better than being on his own, but his still mind raced. *Where are we going? Where is Gydja? She needs to join the herd too!* Fleygur stuck his nose out and bellowed, *I am here!*

Jones's growls of, "Shut it," every time Fleygur shouted barely registered with him. He continued to shout, shaking his head and almost running into the back of the other horses, who put their ears back at him as their riders scowled at Jones.

"Please slow to a walk," boomed the disembodied voice. "Now, change direction and show fast tölt on the long sides of the track."

They turned around and Fleygur found himself in front of the other horses. He slowed up and tried to turn to stay with them, but as they reached a corner of the track Jones gave Fleygur a hefty boot in the ribs and Fleygur leapt forward into gallop. *If I can't stay with them I'll run back to Gydja,* he thought.

Jones tugged at his mouth with the bit. "Tölt, you stupid horse."

Fleygur shook his head trying to shift the pain from his mouth, but he came back to tölt and tried to listen to Jones's confusing instructions. Just when he thought he was catching up with the other horses, Jones would make him slow down again. Fast, slow, fast, slow. Fleygur wished Jones would make up his mind. He snorted his

67

frustration and tossed his head.

"Thank you riders," said the Speaker's voice. "Please return to walk, while we take the scores from the judges."

The horses in front dropped into walk, and when Jones released his reins, Fleygur gratefully tucked his head in behind them. As the adrenaline seeped away he felt the pain in his back, and the sore in his mouth was throbbing.

*I don't think you've got the hang of this competition thing,* said the jet black horse, as they waited at the end of the track. *Competition?* Fleygur had been so distracted by where Gydja was that the whole class had gone by and he didn't even know they had started!

"And the scores for Anthony Jones..." announced the Speaker, "are...2.3....2.5 and...2."

The other horses snigger-snorted.

"....and a Yellow Card!"

The black horse stopped mid snort, *Sorry mate, didn't realise you had one of THOSE riders.*

*What do you mean?* Fleygur asked, feeling overwhelmed by the whole thing.

*You did very badly,* said the black horse, *but the judges didn't like the way your human rode you, so it's probably not your fault.*

*Sometimes humans make mistakes,* said a palomino horse, sounding a bit defensive, *that happened to my human once and she's a kind rider.*

*True,* said the black horse, *but I daresay she didn't hit you like this little horse's human did.*

"So, that's an Official Judge's warning for 'rough riding' for Mr Jones," concluded the voice.

Jones jumped off and flicked the reins over Fleygur's head.

"Aren't you waiting for the placings Tony?" asked one of the other riders.

"NO," he snapped, storming off the track, dragging Fleygur behind him.

Fleygur's nostrils vibrated quietly as they neared Roger and his dad standing at the side of the track. Roger reached out to take Fleygur's reins, but Jones slapped the boy's hand out of the way as he stormed past them.

"Oi!" Roger's father shouted after him, "There's no need for that!"

As they approached the warm up area Fleygur picked up a familiar human smell. He lifted his head to nicker a greeting to Philippa. Jones followed his gaze and immediately looked away again.

"Um…Tony…," she began. "I think it may help if you—"

"Mind your own business," growled Jones,

"But Tony, the reason you were yellow carded—"

"I don't want to hear it."

"But you really shouldn't use the whip to punish—"

"Just leave me ALONE!" Jones glared at Philippa, and then, tugging on Fleygur's reins, he dragged him away.

Back at the trailer Jones tied Fleygur up and began throwing things into the car. Fleygur was hot and itchy, and desperate for a roll. He shifted from one foot to the other and pulled back on his halter rope.

"Cut it out," said Jones, grabbing the saddle from Fleygur's back and chucking it straight in the boot of the car. Fleygur twisted around to look for Gydja, but she was in the other field. He could see the other horses from his class getting a nice cooling wash-down from their humans. The riders were periodically glancing over at Jones, and talking to Philippa, who was wearing one of her deep frowns. Human faces said lots of things, and Fleygur knew that this face meant she was worried.

Then Fleygur caught sight of Roger, marching across the field towards them, and nickered to him, but the boy's father caught up with him and grabbed hold of his arm. Roger tried to pull away, pointing at Fleygur with his free hand, but his dad held him tight.

Fleygur tugged on his halter again, but Jones untied him, turned him roughly to the bottom of the ramp, and thwacked the ground behind him with the whip. Fleygur jumped forward, and before he knew it he was inside the stable-on-wheels and Jones slammed the ramp shut. Fleygur was still sweaty and sticky, but they were off home. He managed a farewell whinny as they bounced off the show ground.

*Goodbye Little One*, came Gydja's distant reply.

## Chapter 10
**Back Home**

The trailer finally trundled into the yard at home and Jones lowered the ramp.

*I'm home,* called Fleygur jogging down the ramp. Beanie and the other horses whinnied a welcome. Jones turned him out in the field and Fleygur dropped straight down for a really long roll, all the way over onto both sides to easy his itching and tired muscles.

Jinks nickered softly as Fleygur got up, and wandered over to offer a mutual groom. Fleygur was glad of the welcome home, and stood happily scratching Jinks's shoulder with his teeth, as Jinks scratched his.

*How did you do?* Jinks asked, *I don't see any rosettes?*

*I think Jones got a yellow one,* Fleygur said.

This being a sports horse thing was much harder than Fleygur thought it would be, but it was what Jones wanted, and he was going to do his best. His mum's farewell lingered in his mind, *a good riding horse is one that can do what its human wants,* she had said. *That's our job, and horses from this farm make the best riding horses, my Little Viking Horse, so you will be the best too.*

After a few days, just when Fleygur was just getting the hang of doing nothing again, Jones reappeared with his halter.

"Right you," he said. "We're having another go at this. It's one month until the competition in Germany, and come hell-or-high-water I am going to get you going round that Oval Track in a sensible fashion."

Fleygur turned his head away as Jones approached, but his halter was slipped over carefully enough. Fleygur followed Jones to the yard, just in time to see Roger free-wheeling into the yard on his bike. Fleygur's nose vibrated as he nickered *hello* to the boy.

"Finished school already?" Jones asked him.

Roger glanced up, clearly taken aback by Jones's friendly tone. "Yeah. Half-day teacher training," he said.

"Okay. You can watch me train, before you do your chores," said Jones. "Maybe, in the school holidays, you can help out with training too, if your father agrees."

"Really?" said Roger, his eyes widening. "Dad won't mind, he's at work most of the time anyway."

"Sure, I used to help my mother...," Jones

broke off abruptly, like he'd caught himself letting his guard down. "Get the gate will you," he snapped.

Roger opened the gate, his eyes searching Jones's face for some sort of explanation.

*I can't work Jones out, but maybe Roger can,* Fleygur thought. But Jones had closed off again, and though he let Roger stay and watch, he didn't speak to him for the rest of that training session.

Training with Jones remained calmer for the next few weeks. There was no more 'going for a blast' along the bridleways, no flat out gallop or super-fast tölting on the long wide bridleway towards home, and absolutely no clattering into the yard in full tölt and sliding to a stop. Instead they went round and round and round on the homemade Oval Track in the field next to the yard. At first, while Fleygur was trying to work out what was required, there was plenty to keep his mind occupied. Ginger, who liked to know everything that was going on, often stood by the fence watching him going round, and he could see Beanie and the others grazing nearby. Sometimes he could see Roger watching from the yard, or if Jones was in a good mood, leaning on the gate. Roger watched a lot, like Ginger did, taking everything in.

Fleygur had worked out the two patterns that Jones was practicing days ago. It wasn't hard.

One was showing each of the gaits in turn - walk, trot, tölt and canter - and other was slow tölt, then fast tölt then slow tölt again, and then, super-fast tölt all the way round. Jones seemed happy that Fleygur anticipated the change of gait for each class.

"Look at that!" Jones shouted to Roger one day, when he was being particularly friendly. "He knows exactly what to do. If he carries on like this I'll start training the Flying Pace after the next competition."

At the end of the session Jones hopped off, and threw the reins to Roger. "Sort him out," he said.

Fleygur liked it when Roger 'sorted him out.' He didn't just blast him with the freezing water like Jones did. He started by hosing his legs gently, and then worked the hose up his body, allowing Fleygur to get used to the water, and enjoy its cooling effect. Then Roger gave him a lovely massage with the red nobbly bar. The boy knew his favourite itchy spots, and where he was stiff, carefully rubbing until Fleygur felt the knots in his muscles unwind. This boy listened to horses and Fleygur liked him.

"All done," said Roger, as he finished Fleygur's massage, "Wish I could come to Germany with you, but Dad said flat out no. I've got to go to school, and besides," he lowered his voice to a conspiratorial whisper, "he says he doesn't trust Mr Jones. Says he's too 'vol-a-tile.' I think it means like unpredictable. Don't we know it!"

Fleygur didn't know what Germany was, but he understood that Roger was sharing something with him. He lipped at Roger's hands and frisked his pockets for treats. Roger ruffled his mane and slipped him a piece of carrot. Fleygur munched happily and they stood together for a while, quietly breathing in time.

But there were many days when Roger was not there. Fleygur missed him, seeking out his scent around the yard, sniffing the rope, or the gloves that Roger had left on a stable door. Today, was one of those days, and Jones had brought Fleygur in for another training session. Fleygur liked to be with his friends, places he knew, and he liked routine, but right now he was getting very bored. Slow tölt, fast tölt, slow tölt, round and round. Fleygur was fit, his black coat shone and he was ready to be a champion sport horse now, just as Jones wanted him to be. But mostly he was ready to be somewhere else. Anywhere rather than going round and round, and round on this track, over and over again, day after day.

"Come on Fleygur," said Jones, "Where's your fire gone? You should be fit enough by now. We are off to Germany tomorrow."

They slowed to a walk and Fleygur dropped

his head with a big snort.

"I've got some new competition mix, I was saving for the show," said Jones. "I'll add that to your feed tonight. That should pep you up a bit."

Jones put Fleygur in one of the stables that evening, inside the big barn, next to where Ginger and Beanie spent each night. Jinks and Lina called to him from the field for a while, but Fleygur was too busy scoffing down his feed to answer them. He was enjoying the new flavours, and the extra big portion, 'to make sure he was fighting fit in the morning,' Jones had said. But the extra big feed sat heavily in Fleygur's stomach that night, and he felt very uncomfortable.

By the next morning Fleygur had belly ache. He was hot and he felt like something sharp was biting in his stomach. He kicked at it with his hind leg but it didn't help. Jones arrived with his halter and Fleygur whipped his head round to point at his belly with his nose, but Jones didn't notice.

"Come on you, no dawdling, we've a long trip ahead," said Jones.

Fleygur sniffed at the travel rug that Jones was holding, where Roger's scent lingered. He lifted his head and looked around, hopeful for a reassuring scratch. The boy would notice that something was wrong, but Roger was not here.

"Come on, on you get," said Jones, giving Fleygur a slap on his rump. Fleygur hesitated on the ramp, but knowing that resisting was no good, he walked into the trailer. Jinks whinnied from the field, but Fleygur felt so unwell that he didn't even bother to nicker to his friend. As they trundled out of the yard he shifted his weight from side to side, and kicked at the sharp pain jabbing in his belly. Last night's feed had not agreed with him, though he had enjoyed every bit of it at the time. Now he felt like something was twisting his insides. The pain spread through his body, and he broke into a sweat.

## CHAPTER 11
### The Storm

By the time Jones stopped for a break Fleygur was feeling very sorry for himself. He drank from the bucket of water that Jones offered, but he really wanted out, he needed to roll. Fleygur stamped on the floor and jabbed his nose in the air, then kicked again at the pain in his belly, but no matter what he did Jones just didn't seem to get that something was wrong. *He's just not paying any attention*, thought Fleygur. He bobbed his head vigorously and kicked at his belly again, but it did no good.

"We've a long way to go yet," Jones said, and slammed the door shut, leaving Fleygur on his own again.

They trundled on for hours and eventually the pain in Fleygur's belly began to ease. When they finally stopped he lifted his tail and pooed. That felt so much better, what ever it was that had been twisting and biting at his insides had gone. He waited, tensed and alert, listening for signs of the door being unbolted. They had been motionless for a long time. He shoved at the haynet with his nose, but although the pain in his belly had gone away, he still didn't feel like eating. He could eat when he got out of here, it must be soon.

Fleygur could taste salty moisture in the air, mixed with dirty oily smells that left a nasty taste in the back of this throat. He flicked his ears at the clanging and banging and unfamiliar voices from outside the trailer. He shifted his weight from one pair of feet to the other, and then arched his neck and dipped his back, to try and stretch his tired muscles. He was tied up so he couldn't lower his head for a proper stretch.

He pawed the floor, anticipating the new paddock that must be waiting outside for him, but instead of the door opening, the car engine started, and then other engines nearby. Slowly they crept forward. Then, he was suddenly tipped backwards and the trailer rattled as they drove up a steep ramp. Fleygur turned his head to peer over his shoulder. The sounds of engines became louder, then echoey, and then the trailer disappeared into a cavernous dark space. A huge lorry pulled up behind them blocking out the light. Fleygur could no longer see the outside world. He bobbed his head and nickered anxiously. He was trapped.

Jones opened the trailer door and heaved a bucket of water inside, fixing it in place with a piece of orange baling twine, like the one that keeps the hay bales together. Then, Jones unclipped the rope from the halter, opened the bar at Fleygur's chest, stepped out of the trailer and shut the door again. Nothing to reassure him, *not a scratch, a word or even a pat!* Fleygur was not tied up now, so there was nothing to stop him lowering his head for that stretch, or moving forwards and backwards, but he was still stuck in the narrow trailer with strange noises all around him. He could sense the presence of other horses nearby and called out to them, but their replies were drowned out by a deep rumble, as the floor beneath him started to vibrate. He snorted in alarm, but was greeted only by a rhythmic thud, thud, thud, as they began to move again. Not the short jerky movements of the trailer on the road, but a gentle sway, first one way then the other. Fleygur's nostrils flared and his heartbeat quickened. This didn't feel right, not right at all.

Slowly Fleygur became accustomed to the motion, and rocking his body gently with the movement, he eventually closed his eyes to doze. He was tired, really tired, but a full proper flat-out-on-the-ground sleep would have to wait until they got where ever it was they were going. Right now he had to make do with dozing.

The air was really stuffy. The constant rocking made his stomach feel strange again, and his mouth was dry. Fleygur dipped his nose into the bucket and sloshed the water, taking some into his mouth. It tasted different from his water at home so he didn't drink it, just held it there for a while and allowed some to dribble out between his lips. He didn't want to eat, he didn't want to drink. He just wanted out.

Suddenly there were voices outside, and he could hear the sound of doors and ramps being opened and closed. Fleygur jerked up his head and nickered, *Who's there?*

"Be quick," someone said, "The wind is getting up. There'll be no passengers allowed below deck until after we dock."

Fleygur stamped his foot and snorted, *Let me out. Let me out.*

The little side door on his trailer was opened and a man stuck his head inside.

"This one looks very sweaty, and he hasn't touched his water."

"Oh, that will be Tony Jones's horse," came a voice from outside.

"He's probably not been on a boat before poor thing. I don't know what idiot agreed to take horses on board tonight. They must have known a storm was on its way, especially a big one like this."

"Is Tony coming down then?" asked the man, with his head still through the door.

"Nah, he's in the bar. Apparently he doesn't like boats. Gets seasick."

The man gave Fleygur a little scratch. "I can't leave this poor fella like this."

"You take your life in your hands if you interfere with Jones's business."

"Well, I can't just leave him!" he said taking some apples pieces from his pocket and offering them to Fleygur. The apples smelled sweet and Fleygur took them gratefully.

"At least he'll have something in him," said the man, closing the door.

Fleygur listened to the footsteps and voices fading away and it was quiet again. Except for the thud, thud, thud, as the waves slapped the side of the boat.

His mouth felt a little better after the apples, and he dipped his nose into the water and drank a little. The coolness felt good, but nothing else did. He was hot and stiff and tired. He dropped his left hip, and with the tip of his foot on the floor he was able to rest one of his hind legs. He lowered his head to doze, but each time he rested a foot, the roll of the boat knocked him off balance.

The roll was getting bigger.

Then suddenly there was a loud slap as a huge wave hit the side of the boat. Fleygur jerked his head up in alarm. Chains and ropes clattered and crashed as the boat lurched from one side, and then to the other. He didn't like being in this little box, something bad was happening and he needed to get out. His heart rate shot up as the adrenaline pumped though his body, preparing him to run. He had to run, he needed to run. He could hear other horses stamping and joined in. Stamp, stamp. *Let me out, let me out!*

Water sloshed out of the bucket and over his front legs as the boat lurched again to the left, and then the right, and then up, and then down. Even over the rumble of the engines, the thud of the waves and the crashing chains, Fleygur could hear the ferocious wind and rain, accompanied by loud claps of thunder.

The pitch and roll was so pronounced now that Fleygur was struggling to stay on his feet. He could hear other horses snorting in alarm, and at least one sounded like he was trying to kick his way out of his box. Every fibre in Fleygur's body was screaming *run!* His hunger and thirst was nothing now, any thoughts of food vanished from his mind. It was dark, he was trapped, and he was terrified.

The boat pitched violently upwards and the bucket broke free, clattering between Fleygur's legs. He reared up in a blind panic smashing his head on the roof of the trailer. As he came down dazed, his knees crumpled and he fell awkwardly, wedged between the central partition and the wall of the trailer.

Fleygur lowered his nose to the floor and gave in to the sway of the storm. His head lolled from side to side and he closed his eyes. He was too exhausted to keep fighting.

*This is it*, thought Fleygur, *I was born in a storm, now I am going to die in one.*

## CHAPTER 12
### Jones the Bully

Sometime in the early hours of the morning the storm began to ease, and Fleygur was able to scramble to his feet. His head ached, and his knees were sore, but he had survived. His belly rumbled. He reached out for some hay, but his mouth was so dry he could barely chew. He nudged the water bucket with his nose, but it was empty. His belly rumbled again.

When the boat finally docked in the harbour there was a hum of activity as the humans were allowed back into the hold. Even Jones put in an appearance, sticking his head through the door.

"Well, he's still standing," said Jones. "We'll be able to get on our way soon enough."

"Don't be an idiot," said a familiar voice. It was the man with the apples. "After that storm all these horses need a good rest, food and water."

"I haven't got time for that nonsense," said Jones, tying Fleygur's rope to the front of the trailer and closing the door. "I'm already a day late. Our first class is tomorrow. I'm on the road as soon as we are allowed off this rust-bucket."

As they rattled down the ramp and on to the road the sweat on Fleygur's body began to cool and he shivered. The sweat rug, designed to wick moisture away, hung uselessly next to him, over the central partition. Yet again, Jones had ignored Fleygur's needs. He was certainly not 'the one' that Fleygur's mother had spoken about, but Jones was Fleygur's human, and it looked like he was stuck with him.

Late in the evening the trailer slowed to a stop, and the engine went quiet. Fleygur could hear voices outside, and the scents of dozens of other horses wafted into his nostrils. Fleygur was exhausted, and thirsty. He wanted out and stamped impatiently. The longer he waited the more frustrated and frightened he became. The last time he had waited like this, the boat, the sea, and the storm had followed.

*I am going to die if I don't get out of here*, he thought. His heart raced, filling his body and mind with the signals to run, and no longer able to contain the feelings stirred up in the storm, he reared up, crashing his front hooves down on the floor and snorting.

"Blimey, have you got a dragon in there?" Someone asked, from outside the trailer.

The ramp was lowered, and Jones untied Fleygur's rope, completely unprepared for the explosion as Fleygur barged him out of the way.

Ripping the rope through Jones's hands Fleygur galloped, then skidded to a halt, spun around on his hind legs and headed off in the opposite direction, looking for a way out of the fenced paddock. *Run, run*, his instincts told him. Fleygur vented his fear in a bucking frenzy, sending clouds of dust swirling up into the air. He dodged several humans who tried and failed, to grab his rope as he bolted between a long row of temporary canvas stables.

"Loose Horse!" someone yelled. "Stand Clear!"

Dozens of humans scattered out of his path as Fleygur snorted, bucked and twisted. Finally, as his fury retreated, Fleygur's senses cleared enough for him to see that he was not about to die. Emotionally and physically spent, Fleygur stood in the corner of the paddock breathing heavily. He dropped his head low.

*I never, ever, want to be inside that stable-on-wheels again*, he snorted.

"Your stable is fourth on the right, in the third row," a man with a clip board said to Jones, and then eyeing Fleygur, "but if you want to let him stretch his legs and let off steam a bit more, there's a small turn out area that way." The man gestured beyond the stables.

"He's stretched his legs already," said Jones, "and I need my bed."

He grabbed Fleygur's rope. Fleygur was too exhausted to resist and quietly followed him, nickering vibrating nose greetings to the rows of horses as he passed, until finally Jones led him into a large stable, with a deep bed of wood shavings, a bucket of water and a haynet stuffed with sweet smelling hay. Fleygur explored the small space, sniffing at the strange thin walls made of canvass, that flapped slightly in the breeze. After a full inspection he concluded that it all seemed safe, and breathed out deeply, letting all the muscles that he had held tight for two days relax for the first time.

*Quite some entrance*, said a horse from the stable opposite Fleygur. *You should save your energy for the competition.*

Fleygur lifted his head over the stable door and greeted the handsome red horse with a quiet nicker.

*I'm Magnus*, said a pinto horse next to him, *and that red horse knows his stuff. He's Kraftur frá Bringu. He's a world champion sport horse.*

*We are all sport horses here, Magnus*, said Kraftur, *even though this little horse looks more like he needs a good long rest.*

Fleygur liked Kraftur, he seemed to be gentle and wise, like his friend Gydja.

*I'm to be a sport horse too*, Fleygur said, *my human has been training me, but he doesn't know horse-talk—*"

Fleygur flinched as Jones reappeared suddenly at the stable door.

"Come on, you have to be vet-checked, he said. "'It has to be the day you arrive, no exceptions', according to the bossy-boots with the clip-board," Jones grumbled.

He led Fleygur back through the row of stables. Horses' heads appeared over the stable doors as he walked by, but he wasn't allowed to stop and greet any of them properly. They crossed the fenced paddock where Fleygur had let rip with his bucking tantrum, and arrived at a small fenced area.

A woman with a clipboard and pen gestured them towards a space in a row of horses, all waiting quietly with their humans. A vet was moving slowly down the line, checking each horse carefully. Fleygur knew the particular smell of vets, and tensed a little as she came closer. It's not that the vets he'd met weren't kind. They were mostly pretty good at horse-talk, but sometimes they did unexpected things, like stick a needle in you, or wedge your mouth open and file your teeth!

"He seems a bit dehydrated," said the Vet pinching the skin on Fleygur's face and squinting at him. Fleygur snuffled at her hand, she didn't smell of treats but she was gentle, like Roger was.

"What do you expect!" snapped Jones, "We're just off the boat."

"Has he had a fall?" the Vet asked, brushing lightly at Fleygur's knees. "There's a slight graze here."

Fleygur bobbed his head as he felt Jones's temper begin to rise.

"No, he hasn't! What he has done is behave like a complete idiot when we arrived, bucking around the place. He's just dirty for goodness sake!" Jones's voice was getting louder with every word. "He's a horse, not a prize sculpture. Are you going to examine every hair on his head?"

"No, Mr Jones, but there are certain checks that the rules require." She was running her hands down Fleygur's back. He flinched when she reached the sore spot where his saddle dug in. The Vet drew breath to speak, but before she could start Jones drew himself up, and spoke slowly, in a dangerously quiet voice, "He fidgets. He always does."

There was a pause as Jones and the Vet looked at each other.

*If they were horses,* Fleygur thought, *they would squeal at each other now.* But after a moment the vet looked away. She seemed shaken by the silent confrontation.

"I just need to look in his mouth," she said sliding her finger into the side of Fleygur's mouth and lifting his head to peer inside.

"Have you quite finished?" growled Jones.

Fleygur tried to pull away, so he could put some distance between himself and the bubbling volcano he could sense building in Jones.

"Just one moment, I can't quite see in…," said the Vet, losing her grip on Fleygur's jaw as he stepped back.

"RIGHT! That's enough!" said Jones. "You ARE done now!"

The Vet's face flushed red as she quickly finished making some marks on her clipboard. She handed Jones a slip of paper, and walked away.

Jones read from the slip, "Fit to compete," and scrunched the paper into his breast pocket. "Good, now you'd better behave tomorrow. This is my big break."

Fleygur didn't feel fit to compete. His belly was still sore and grumbly, his head hurt and his knees were bruised. He really needed Roger here, with his nobbly bar, to give him a nice massage, but all he had was Jones, who couldn't horse-talk at all.

Back in his temporary stable, Fleygur munched on some hay for a while, then sank to his knees, in spite of the soreness, and lay down in the inviting thick bedding. He could doze standing up of course, but he had not been able to lie down since they left home two days ago. He needed a proper flat-out sleep. Fleygur's eyes flickered closed. His bottom lip dropped open, and as he began to drift into sleep his head slowly lowered until his nose rested on the floor. Balanced on his nose his head dropped from one side to the other, until finally he let go, and lay flat out in the stable, breathing deeply. The sounds of the other horses drifted away.

As the thud, thud, thud of the boat's engine reverberated around his head, a nervous nicker trickled from his nose.

## CHAPTER 13
### Judged

It was barely light when the yard was transformed from rows of peacefully dozing horses to a hive of activity, as horses were led this way and that. Fleygur stood with his head over the stable door trying to greet each horse as it passed. Some returned his nicker, but others were so preoccupied by their own fears that they barely noticed him as they pranced and jogged by.

*Don't waste your energy. It's going to be a hot day,* said Kraftur frá Bringu, as he ambled past, following his rider who was on foot in front of him.

Fleygur thought Kraftur looked so cool, following his human all calm and relaxed. He didn't seem at all bothered by the commotion of the show. Kraftur's red coat shimmered in the rising sunlight, and as the sun climbed above the high walls of the nearby stadium the air temperature rose sharply. The night moisture evaporated rapidly from the ground, creating an eerie mist, and the warm air closed in around Fleygur.

All of the horses in his row had gone now,

and Fleygur paced up and down in his stable. Alone, in a confined space, he fretted and tossed his head. Finally Fleygur heard the tap-tap-tap of Jones's whip on his boot. He spun around to the stable door and let out an excited whicker at the thought of being with the other horses again.

"Well, that's a first," said Jones, "You've never greeted me like that before. Maybe we're getting somewhere." He ruffled Fleygur's mane and slipped on the halter.

As he walked from the stable Fleygur paused to stretch out his stiff back leg. There was a loud click from his ankle joint. It felt good, but what he really wanted was a roll, or a fast canter with several twisty bucks thrown in. That would soon loosen him up. But Jones remained oblivious to Fleygur's stiffness and just gave him a quick brush and tacked him up.

Jones might be thinking they were 'getting somewhere,' but that almost affectionate ruffle of his mane earlier didn't convince Fleygur. It didn't matter if Jones said something nice, or gave him a scratch or a pat. None of it mattered if the man couldn't feel when something was wrong with his horse; and Jones didn't seem much better with humans either.

*But I will do my best,* thought Fleygur, *because that's what good riding horses do.*

As they made their way to the warm up area

Fleygur could hear a muffled roar coming from the stadium and he snorted nervously. Huge dark clouds were forming overhead. Fleygur's heart quickened and he jogged, quickly breaking into a sweat. He saw Magnus, the pinto from his stable row, and tried to swerve in his direction. Jones gave a sharp pull on the reins, and a stinging thwack on Fleygur's thigh. The horses nearest him jumped sideways and their riders frowned at Jones. A couple of the humans standing around the warm up area pointed at Jones and Fleygur, and whispered to each other. Fleygur couldn't help but notice that the other riders were calm and quiet with their horses, but he could hear Jones huffing and puffing on his back, and he was constantly shuffling in the saddle and throwing Fleygur off balance.

When they entered the stadium Fleygur's ears were filled with a deafening roar. He skipped sideways and tried to turn. He was sure this roar must belong to some huge horse-eating monster. His heart raced as adrenaline pumped into his veins preparing him for the fight of his life, but the other horses on the track seemed unperturbed, and Jones was still squeezing him forwards with his legs.

*Don't worry, it's just humans cheering*, said Magnus, tölting passed him. *You'll get used to it. It spooks all the youngsters at first.*

Fleygur picked up on Magnus's confidence, and feeling a little bolder he quickly followed him onto the track. Jones pulled hard on the reins for no reason that Fleygur could understand, so he threw his head about trying to pull the restricting reins from Jones's hands. Jones responded with two sharp pulls with the reins, jabbing the bit painfully into Fleygur's gums. The roar subsided and there was booing from some people in the crowd, and then quiet as the class commenced.

Fleygur felt a warm sticky trickle on his tongue.

He was determined not to lose sight of the other horses and settled into his tölt, with Magnus in plain view in front of him. The quiet was broken occasionally with a shower of applause from the crowd. The adrenaline slowly flowed out of Fleygur's system, taking his spirit with it. The storm clouds had blown over, but the stuffy oppressive heat remained, and it sapped his remaining strength. Fleygur slowed. It was all catching up with him, the colic in his belly before they left home, the hours in the trailer, the storm. He had been all night in that stuffy stable, when what he needed was a good roll and to stretch his legs in the cool night breeze. He was bruised and drained. He slowed some more, and dropped out of tölt back to walk.

Jones's response was swift and hard, THWACK, THAWCK! The whip stung on his rump and Fleygur responded instinctively, his head went down and his bum up, BUCK, BUCK! The crowd gasped.

Jones clamped his legs on hard and held Fleygur's head up in the air with the reins. It hurt, but he couldn't keep fighting, so Fleygur went back into tölt, and tried hard to keep up with the other horses, who were now lapping him on the track. But his energy was gone, his hooves felt dragged down with heavy weights, and he could barely lift them more than a few inches from the ground.

As the class ended a voice boomed from the speakers, "Anthony Jones and Herdís Björnsdóttir, please report for an equipment check."

Magnus came alongside Fleygur. *That's me and you, getting checked over,* he said brightly, still excited from the class. Fleygur could feel Magnus's excitement, but he didn't share it. He could hardly put one foot in front of the other. As they made their way to the Equipment Check Enclosure Fleygur's head dropped close to the ground.

"Your horse is very tired," said Herdís, Magnus's rider. Jones said nothing and a tense silence followed.

"Please dismount." The Equipment Judge instructed the riders.

Fleygur was motionless as the Judge checked the length of Jones's whip, and took the hoof-boots off his front feet and weighed them.

*It's to stop the humans cheating,* Magnus told him. *Some humans will do anything to make us lift our legs higher and get a better score.*

Fleygur could believe it, especially of Jones. He was glad that Jones hadn't discovered these cheats yet, or he was sure he would have used them. But Fleygur was too tired to respond to Magnus so he just stood quietly as the Judge slid two fingers under his nose band. She gave a short nod, but when she unbuckled it, and Fleygur stretched open his mouth, a thin trickle of blood pooled on his bottom lip.

The Judge, the Vet, Jones, and Herdís Björnsdóttir watched as it dripped onto the dusty floor.

## CHAPTER 14
### I'm Not Going in There!

The scores for the class were being read out by the Speaker, but no-one in the Judges Enclosure was listening. The Judge gestured to the Vet and she stepped forward, glancing at Jones. She gently opened Fleygur's mouth and peering inside, she winced. In a small tight voice she said, "There is a large laceration to the upper left bar of the jaw and...," she hesitated, and her face flushed red, "...signs of a burst ulcer," she sighed.

The Judge shot her a look. "How was that not picked up at Vet Check?"

The Vet glanced at Jones, her face flushing again.

"Well," said the Judge "That's a Red Card, Mr Jones, your horse is bleeding!"

While the Judge spoke into a crackling radio the Vet sprayed something into Fleygur's mouth and whispered, "I'm so sorry boy."

Fleygur puckered his upper lip at the strange taste in his mouth. The stinging on his jaw subsided. Finally, someone had noticed his pain. The Vet had a nice voice, and was gently scratching behind his ear. Fleygur lent his head into her body, and breathed out his relief.

"A further announcement on the last class," announced the Speaker. "Mr Anthony Jones, from Great Britain, has been disqualified."

There was the distant sound of cheering from the Stadium.

"They don't like cruelty, Mr Jones," said the Judge, "and neither do I! That was appalling riding. Your horse is clearly exhausted and unprepared for this level of competition." Her voice was rising along with her eyebrows. Fleygur knew this meant she was angry, but he also knew it wasn't directed at him. "If it was up to me," she continued, "you wouldn't be allowed to ride in competitions at all, not until you learnt to show some respect for your horse. It's supposed to be a partnership!"

*A partnership? Not with Jones*, Fleygur thought.

The Judge glared at Jones, then turned and walked away.

The Vet drew herself up in front of Jones. "Your horse needs rest, water and then some LIGHT exercise," she said, "Here's the medication for the laceration in his mouth, and he must NOT be ridden with a bit until the wound is completely healed."

The only thing the Vet didn't mention was food. Fleygur was sure his treatment needed to

101

include extra food.

"Do you understand me Mr Jones?"

"Yes!" he snapped, as he took Fleygur's reins from the Vet and led him away.

Fleygur was glad to be back at the stable block with the other horses. Jones was sullen, and none of the other riders appeared to be talking to him, but at least he seemed to be following the Vet's instructions. His water was freshened, and Fleygur heard the Yard Manager say that he had been allocated extra time in the turn out area, where there was still some grass. Grass! Lovely juicy green stuff. Hay was good, but only when there was no grass. Besides the hay was dry and harsh on his sore mouth.

It was four days before the Vet cleared Fleygur for travel. Fleygur actually felt pretty good after just one days rest, but he wasn't complaining. Jones had put in an appearance daily, to change his water and apply the medication, or to walk him to the turn out paddock, but the rest of the time he got to hang out, roll, relax and eat. Fleygur became accustomed to the buzz of the competition, and the warmth of the sun. He had begun to think that this sport horse thing was over rated. To be a good riding horse was enough for him. He just needed to find a human who could horse-talk, and understood his every need. Just someone like that, how hard could it be?

On the morning of the fourth day, as Jones led him towards the fenced paddock, Fleygur spotted the trailer parked in the middle and froze. He was expecting to go to the turn-out area, not to be confronted with the stable-on-wheels. Jones tugged on the rope and Fleygur stepped forward, but as they reached the bottom of the ramp Fleygur stopped again. The dark enclosed space at the top of the ramp terrified him. He trembled at the thought of being inside.

Jones leaned against the rope and pulled.

Fleygur planted his four hooves and leaned back. The halter dug into his head but still he did not move. The pain on his head reminded him of being in the belly of the boat as it was thrown from the top of one wave to the next. He could not go there again. He would not. It was as if the adrenalin pumping in his body had poured down into his feet and glued them firmly to the ground.

Jones went red in the face, but suddenly, he let go of the rope. Fleygur stood with the lead-rope on the floor in front of him breathing quickly, while Jones glared at him. Then, just as if someone had walked behind him and flipped a switch, Jones said, "Right!" and marched off. Fleygur didn't know what to do, left with his lead-rope dangling. He looked around, his eyes wide, feeling uncertain.

When Jones returned he had a long rope, and

a whip.

"Do you need help loading?" asked a young man, walking towards them.

"NOPE," Jones snapped, and the man moved away again, looking back over his shoulder with a frown. Jones picked up the lead-rope. Fleygur swished his tail anxiously, but Jones didn't try to pull him in. Fleygur watched as Jones fixed the end of the long rope to one side of the trailer, took the rope around the back of Fleygur's legs, and threaded the other end through a metal eyelet on the other side of the trailer. Then, with a snap, he suddenly pulled the rope and it slapped against Fleygur's legs. Fleygur's head shot up, and he tried to kick out behind, but there was nothing to kick. He could not go backwards now, but he was not going forwards. Not ever.

Jones flicked the whip on the ground behind Fleygur and pulled the rope tight on his legs. Fleygur flinched at the sound, but all four hooves stayed where they were. Jones raised the whip again, growling, "You're getting on that trailer, or one of us dies today!" Jones brought the whip down again, but this time harder, and directly onto Fleygur's rump. Fleygur reared up at the sudden sting, and tried to spin around, but Jones was yelling and bringing the whip down repeatedly on Fleygur's back and legs. Fleygur panicked, he had to get away. As he clattered around on the ramp, trying to evade the whip, one hoof slipped off the side and he stumbled to his knees. Frightened and feeling vulnerable, he scrambled to his feet quickly, but Jones leapt onto the ramp and lashed at him with the whip.

"You stupid animal." Spittle flew from Jones's mouth, "Get on there, or you are MEAT!"

Fleygur could hear other humans shouting, and saw two men running into the paddock. In his panic Fleygur crashed up the ramp to get away from the stinging blows, and right into the trailer. Jones triumphantly slammed the rear bar in place, just as a familiar figure charged into Jones almost knocking him off his feet. It was the apples-man from the boat.

"Lay off that horse, you thug!" the man yelled, wrestling the whip from Jones's hands. The two men fell into the dirt struggling. A woman appeared at the front ramp and stood at Fleygur's head, talking to him calmly, but she was drowned out by the shouting from the fight outside. The fighting men fell against the side of the trailer and Fleygur flinched at the bang. Alarmed, he stamped his hooves on the floor and arched his head around, just in time to see the apples-man running away, with Jones in hot pursuit, waving the whip.

Moments later Jones reappeared, and grabbing the woman with the soft voice by the arm, he hauled her off the trailer and slammed the doors closed.

"You can all go to HELL!" he screamed.

## Chapter 15
### Abandoned

A few hours later the salty scent of the sea reached Fleygur's nostrils and he sniffed the air anxiously. The banging and clanging at the dockside jangled his nerves, and he snorted fearfully as the trailer was towed up the ramp and into the belly of the boat. Fleygur trembled as the boat set sail, but this time there was no storm, just a gentle sway, to and fro. Slowly, very slowly, he started to relax, and dozed for the rest of the journey.

When they finally arrived home Jones was grim faced and silent. He barely looked at Fleygur as he unloaded him. Fleygur flinched as Jones reached for his head collar, but Jones wasn't rough or cruel this time, just cold and distant. Fleygur was glad, he wasn't going to forget that beating for a long time. He was still sore from the bruises he sustained on the boat trip out, and stiff from the demands of the competition, but these were nothing to the beating. The bruises would heal but he would be quite happy if Jones never came near him ever again. He would just be glad to be back with the other horses, where he understood the rules.

But as he jogged out of the trailer Fleygur realised this wasn't a part of the farm that he knew. They were parked near to an old sandstone barn that had seen better days. A faded oak-panelled door was hanging on to its doorframe with one rusty hinge, and the roof had caved in long ago. Ivy wound its way up and out through the open doorway and onto the charcoaled black beams, which were sticking up into the air like the ribs of a large animal picked clean by scavengers. It was obvious that the blaze that had collapsed the roof was an age old, but Fleygur could still smell traces of the fire, and he eyed the barn cautiously. Fire was dangerous. Fire was something to stay away from, at all costs.

His familiar yard was somewhere near though, he could hear the dogs barking, and the scents of his herd-mates were on the breeze. He nickered anxiously as Jones took him past the burnt-out barn, and down a long grassy lane that looked like no-one had walked it for years. No horse had been here for a very long time, Fleygur was sure of that. There were no droppings to smell, and the grass was un-grazed. A small fallen tree, covered in moss, lay across the track and Jones stepped over it. Fleygur hesitated, but a sharp jab on the halter from Jones made it clear that this was not negotiable. Fleygur didn't understand what was happening, why wasn't Jones taking him back to his herd? Fleygur's nostrils flared as he whinnied for his friends.

"Shut it," said Jones, giving another yank on the rope. At the end of the lane Jones hauled open an old wooden gate and turned him into the field.

"You can stay here, where I don't have to look at you!" he growled. Then he chained up the gate, turned on his heels and walked away. Some of the tension trickled out of Fleygur's body as he watched Jones disappear up the lane without a backward glance.

*That's a very bad man,* thought Fleygur. Just the idea of being close to Jones made Fleygur tense, but being on his own was nearly as bad. He scanned the field. There were bright green hawthorn hedges to be nibbled, a water trough, a huge oak tree to stand under and swish flies away with his tail, and a metal gate on the opposite side through to a narrow lane.

*Maybe that would be a good place to harass passing humans for treats,* Fleygur thought. And there was lots and lots of long lush grass. He was usually contained within electric fences, his access to grass restricted, so Fleygur felt a little excited. He cantered and bucked his way to the middle of the field. It would take him weeks to eat all this. He lowered his head to nibble the grass, but snapped it up again just as quickly. Eating always made him feel calmer, but he didn't like being on his own.

He whinnied, *Hello? Where are you?* and pricked his ears. Nothing.

He couldn't see or hear any other horses. His heartbeat quickened and he whinnied again, louder this time, *I am here, where are you?* Still nothing.

This was not right, horses were meant to be together. It wasn't safe to be on your own, there had to be others. He set off at a brisk trot, tossing his head. He stretched forward his nose and bellowed right from his belly, *Helloooo! Answer me!* He stopped stock still, ears pricked forward. There! There was an answering whinny, it was in the distance, but there it was! He bellowed again and this time he got two replies, from Ginger and Beanie.

*We hear you. We are here.*

Fleygur cantered around the field tossing his head in frustration and calling, but there was no way to get to them, and eventually Ginger and Beanie stopped answering his calls.

Standing alone in the field breathing hard, sweat tricking down his chest and the backs of his legs, a quiet, half-hopeless nicker escaped Fleygur's lips. He was alone. He lowered his head to graze again and his heart rate slowed, but he still didn't feel right. Every few minutes he snapped his head up, looked around and listened, flickering his ears trying to catch any sound of his friends, or anyone. He paced every inch of the field, checking the hedges and gates, breathing in the scents and tastes, and taking the odd nibble of the goosegrass and cowslips at the edges of the field.

Days went by and hardly anyone passed along the lane. Once or twice he caught sight of Jones at the grassy lane gate, but he never came in, and Fleygur was certainly not going to walk over to him.

Days turned to a week, and then two. Fleygur grew round and fat from the rich and plentiful grass. Occasionally a car whizzed past, and once, a woman sitting high above the hedge on a tractor, looked across at him as she bounced down the lane. The tractor slowed briefly by the gate, and Fleygur lifted his head from grazing to look back at the woman. He was about to trot over to the gate when she moved off again. He was lonely. It was not natural for a horse to be on his own, with no field-mates to share look out duties, to let off steam with a good chase around the field, or play 'who's the boss' fighting. With no-one for a spot of mutual grooming, Fleygur had to make do with finding things to scratch on to relieve his itching, like the metal gate.

One day he was just settling into a good scratch on the gate when something unexpected happened. Fleygur had reversed a few steps until he felt the gate touch his bum, then widened the stance of his back legs, leaned back, rocked side to side and ...*ahh! That's it, that's the spot.*

Then he heard hoof-beats on the lane. He stiffened and pricked his ears to locate the direction. He whipped around and nickered a greeting to two big horses coming down the lane towards him. He didn't know them, but any company was good right now. As they drew level with the gate he called again, and the two riders glanced at him, but carried on chatting as they rode on by. One of the horses had a sneaky look in Fleygur's direction, but these horses knew their job, and knew better than to try and stop to greet another horse while out with their humans.

Fleygur didn't want to be on his own again and galloped alongside the hedge after them. He could hear their hoof-beats quicken a little as they heard him coming, but as he splashed into the muddy wet corner of the field, they continued down the lane and out of sight. He spun around to gallop out his frustration, and as he turned, his left front hoof sunk deep into the mud. Fleygur tensed the muscles in his hind quarters and sprang forward, but something buried in the mud had caught on his metal shoe. The force of his leap was so strong that as his foot lifted the shoe twisted and tore away, exposing three nails. The pull had unbalanced him and he stumbled forward. He just managed to stay on his feet, but as his left foot hit the ground again one of the nails punctured the soft sole of his foot. Pain shot through his leg.

Fleygur wasn't sure what had just happened but he was unable to put his foot down, and he couldn't walk with the twisted shoe still partly attached to his hoof. He waited, his foot throbbing. After the boat trip, and the beating, and then being abandoned Fleygur didn't think it could get much worse, but it seemed he was wrong. He had once thought he would be the best of all riding horses, with his human, who knew his every need, by his side. A true partnership, but now? Now he was just a fat lonely pony who couldn't even walk. No use to anyone. He tried to shut himself off from the pain, gradually sinking into a daze. He didn't move, his breathing slowed and his eyes drooped. Nothing existed but him, and the dull ache in his foot.

## CHAPTER 16
### Found!

More than an hour passed when Fleygur became aware of a figure at the metal gate. He hadn't seen the boy arrive but there he was, his bicycle propped against the hedge. It was Roger! Roger glanced around, then climbed over the gate and started running towards Fleygur.

Fleygur wanted to greet him, but his mind was numbed by the pain, and although his nose vibrated as Roger drew near, Fleygur couldn't manage a proper nicker. The boy slowed, his face wrinkled with concern.

"What's up, Fleygur?" said Roger, reaching out a hand to Fleygur's nose, and then up to his forehead to give it a rub. "Jones said you'd gone to the pet-food factory! I knew he was lying, but I couldn't find where he'd put you. Then, Joan at the farm next door said she'd seen you."

Slowly Roger ran his hand down Fleygur's shoulder and lifted his foot. "Ah, now I see the problem," he said. "Need to get that shoe off." Putting Fleygur's foot down carefully, he ruffled Fleygur's mane and pulled a tool from a leather pouch on his belt. "Lucky for you, I never go anywhere without this, anywhere except school that is." Roger organised the multi-tool into a pair of pliers, lifted Fleygur's foot again and took hold of the shoe. Then he stopped. "Mm, I'd better not," he said, "Jones will go mad." He lowered Fleygur's foot and gave him a quick scratch. "You wait here, boy. I'll get help."

Fleygur had been standing quietly, relaxed in the boy's presence, but as he watched him go he let out a quiet nicker. Roger turned and smiled at him. "Don't worry boy, I'll be back."

When Roger reappeared along the grassy lane, Jones was just a few steps behind him. Fleygur watched them approach and swished his tail anxiously as Jones came closer. He had a strong urge to run, but he had closed himself down to cope with the pain in his foot, and it was hard to summon the energy to move. Anyway, the boy was coming too and Fleygur had a good feeling about that. Roger reached him first and gave him a reassuring rub on his forehead. "He hasn't moved at all," he said to Jones, "but I am sure it's just because of the twisted shoe."

Jones lifted Fleygur's foot and expertly removed the shoe with Roger's pliers.
"Whatever it is, it better not be costing me anything," he said. "Good money after bad with this horse." Jones let Fleygur put his foot down

for moment and then picked it up again, brushing off the soil for a closer inspection. "Look at this," he said to Roger, "a nail has gone right through the sole. It's almost certain to get infected. That's all I need, this horse is a waste of space at the best of times." Jones pulled the nail out, let Fleygur's foot drop and handed the tool back to the boy. "Now he's going to cost me time and money. It's a shame he didn't do worse, at least I could have had him shot and claimed on the insurance."

Jones must have said something bad, because Fleygur felt the boy stiffen and his heart rate increase.

"I'll look after him," Roger said quickly. Fleygur was feeling a little better with the nail out, and now he could get his foot down properly he quietly stepped away from Jones and closer to his friend Roger. He tucked his head in behind the boy and gently snuffled his pockets. It felt good to breathe in the boy's scent, even if he had no treats today. Roger reached one hand behind his back and tickled Fleygur's nose, but his attention was on Jones. "Just tell me what I need to do," he said, "he'll be no bother to you, I'll do everything."

Jones was looking at Roger with a slightly vague expression on his face, like he was figuring something out in his head. Fleygur was glad the boy was between him and Jones.

"Okay," said Jones eventually, "Come up to

the house in about an hour and I'll give you the med kit. Get him fixed, and I'll see what's to be done with him."

As Jones strode away Roger turned to wrap his arms around Fleygur's neck and buried his face in his mane for a moment, then he crouched down in front of him and blew softly into Fleygur's nostrils. Fleygur breathed in the boy's scent and blew back onto his face. It was good to sense him again, and to say hello properly, horse-style.

Later that afternoon Fleygur was standing at the metal gate when a big black car pulled up in the gateway and Roger hopped out. A man leaned out of the drivers side window.

"You sure you know what you are doing?" he said to the boy.

"Yes, Dad, Jones explained, and I looked it up in Mum's Vet Book," Roger replied.

"And you are sure he's is okay with this, he's not a man to pick a fight with. I can't believe he'd let an eleven-year-old boy take care of one of his prize horses!"

"I'm nearly twelve," Roger said quickly, "Anyway Jones said he didn't give two hoots about this horse, but if I could save him time and money, he might let me help out at the yard full time in the summer holidays, not just brushing and shovelling cra...cleaning up." His words came out in a rush. "I want to work with horses, you know I do. Mum did and I want to."

Roger took a bucket from the back of the truck and lifted it over the gate. Fleygur and Roger's father watched as he took off the lid and poured in some salt. "Can you hold his halter, while I put his foot in." Roger asked.

"Okay," said his father getting out of the car. He was a solidly built man with big shoulders and sky-blue eyes like Roger's, that gazed fondly on his son. He felt calm, *like the boy*, thought Fleygur, the sort of nice kind human that horses liked to be near.

"I can't do this with you every day Rog, you are going to have to figure out how to get this stuff here on you own."

"I'll sort it," Roger said, lifting Fleygur's foot and guiding it into the bucket.

*Oww that's HOT*, thought Fleygur, and snatched it up again.

"Easy, boy," Roger said, and gently pushed it back down, giving Fleygur a piece of carrot. Fleygur forgot about the hot water while he munched on the carrot. He liked carrot, well, he liked any food really, but carrots had that satisfying crunch, and they were sweet. After a few minutes his foot felt uncomfortable again, and he lifted it out of the bucket. Roger pushed it back and gave him another piece of carrot. *Okay, he thought, I get this. I put my foot in the bucket and I get carrot. I can do that.*

"I told you he was a smart horse," Roger said, "I can do it on my own now."

"Okay, I'll leave you to it, but you give me a shout if it looks like it's getting worse. Last thing I need now is Tony Jones breathing down my neck about you ruining one of his sports horses. Or you missing school again!"

As his father's car disappeared down the lane Roger checked his watch. "Right, that should do it," he said. He lifted and dried Fleygur's foot with an old towel, and squeezed some cream into the small hole left by the nail. Then he bandaged the foot and wrapped the whole thing in sticky black gaffer tape. He let Fleygur put his foot back down, and stepped back to take a look.

"Well, it looks pretty naff, but it should keep it clean and dry like Jones said." Roger scratched Fleygur behind his ear.

Early the next morning Fleygur was waiting by the gate when Roger arrived on his bike, with a pushchair tied behind, cradling a bucket of water. "I told Dad I would find a way, and I did!" Roger said with a big grin on his face. "I think some of the water sloshed out, but there's still enough." He hauled the bucket over the gate. The boy seemed really pleased with himself, though Fleygur wasn't sure why. He couldn't really understand what all this fuss with the hot water was about, but as long as it involved carrots, he was fine with it.

As Roger wrapped the freshly cleaned wound with the gaffer tape, he sighed, "I guess I'd better get to school," he said, not sounding at all like he wanted to.

Fleygur didn't blame him, he didn't like going round and round in circles in the school either. It was very boring and hard work. Fleygur was feeling a lot better, but he had some serious eating to make up for and he wandered off to graze as Roger packed up his stuff and headed off.

## CHAPTER 17
### "Please Dad Please!"

Jones had been right about the wound getting infected, and Fleygur started to feel very sorry for himself, hobbling around the field. But Roger didn't let him down. Twice each day he arrived with the bucket of water, and the whole procedure was repeated. Fleygur was an expert now. Lifting his foot before being asked, and standing with his foot in the bucket until Roger told him he could take it out. Roger didn't even put the halter on anymore. There was no need.

*We are a good team*, Fleygur thought. And there was the carrot treat at the end. That helped too.

Fleygur was relieved when after several days some smelly puss oozed out through the small hole in his sole, and the pressure in his foot eased. Shortly after that the infection cleared up and the bandages came off. Roger still came to the field every day, and Fleygur was glad of the company.

He still missed his herd, especially when Roger was away in his school, but he liked the games the boy played with him, most particularly because they often involved treats. All he had to do was figure out what Roger wanted him to do, and when he got it right he got a treat. Sometimes Fleygur would tuck his head in behind Roger's back and follow him as he zig-zagged across the field, and if Roger suddenly dashed off laughing Fleygur would run after him, kicking up his hind legs in excitement as they ran. Sometimes they would just stand together doing nothing. Fleygur liked doing nothing. He could do nothing for hours and hours. Doing nothing was one of Fleygur's favourite things, after eating. Eating was his most favourite thing.

When he wasn't doing nothing, or eating, Fleygur played games with Roger. Roger running, Fleygur chasing. Turning when Roger did, stopping when Roger did, fast, slow, turn, fast, stop. What Roger did Fleygur did. It felt good, it felt safe. He had almost forgotten about Jones's plan for him to be a sport horse. He hadn't even been an ordinary riding horse for weeks.

He had nearly forgotten about Jones too, but all of a sudden there he was, at the grassy lane gate. Fleygur stiffened and pricked his ears towards the gate and Roger followed Fleygur's gaze. Jones had been watching them. As Roger walked towards the gate, Fleygur tucked his head in behind Roger's back and followed. He felt safe behind Roger, he didn't have to scan for danger the whole time. It was a big responsibility being the 'front horse,' and it was good to be able to relax sometimes and just amble along at the back, or even better in the middle, if you were in a proper herd. Being at the back could be risky too, you never knew what might sneak up in your blind spot.

"Well," said Jones, as they drew close.

Fleygur snorted. Even with Roger in front of him, Jones's proximity made him anxious.

"That was quite impressive. You've done a good job there. You could teach some of those tricks to my other horses. People like that kind of stuff when they are buying."

"Buying…?" said Roger.

Roger sounded a little shaky and Fleygur bobbed his head anxiously.

"Are you selling some horses?" asked Roger.

"Yes, and this one first," said Jones waving his arm at Fleygur.

Fleygur felt Roger tense beside him. He wasn't really sure what all this meant, but Roger didn't like it, so he was sure he wouldn't either.

"I've got my eye on a couple of Eventing Horses, big jumpers, a bit of Cross Country, that's what I need," continued Jones. "I'll still be needing a stable-hand, if you're interested."

Roger didn't answer, he just slid his fingers into Fleygur's mane and as they watched Jones stride away up the lane, he gave Fleygur's neck a little squeeze.

Later that afternoon, as the sun was dipping below the tress, Fleygur spotted Roger and his father standing by the road gate, talking earnestly. Fleygur watched for a few moments ears pricked, and then ambled over swishing his tail gently as he walked, nose low to the ground. There was no rush, but maybe Roger had some treats for him.

"We just don't have the money," the boy's father was saying as Fleygur arrived at the gate and snuffled at Roger's open palm.

"What about the money Mum left for me?" Roger asked.

His dad sighed and leant on the gate, "That's for your education. How else am I going to afford college fees on a part-time nurses salary? Money doesn't grow on trees. Anyway, you have Hercules to look after, and a lot of catching up on the school you missed after Mum…" His voice trailed off. They both looked at the ground in an uncomfortable silence.

Fleygur licked the boy's palms, but Roger didn't seem to be paying attention. Roger climbed onto the bottom rung of the gate, leant over and twisted round to look directly into his dad's face. "Please, Dad, PLEASE! I love Hercs, but he's old and I can't ride him anymore. This horse is special. I promise I'll go to school every day, I promise. PLEASE!"

Fleygur had always known he was special, his mum told him he was.

There was a long pause, then suddenly the boy's father straightened up, with his hands resting on the top of the gate. "Okay," he said. 'Wait here."

Roger's eyes widened. Fleygur turned his head with Roger's, as they both watched his father head up the lane towards Jones's farm.

"That was easy!" Roger said, and slid his fingers deep into Fleygur's mane.

As they waited Fleygur could feel the tension oozing from the boy. It was hard to tell if this was excitement or fear and Fleygur bobbed his head anxiously. Roger gave him a little scratch, right in a favourite itchy spot on his neck. "Don't worry Fleygur, Dad will sort it, I'm sure he will. You will be mine at last!"

Half an hour later Roger's father came marching back down the lane, his face stiff and a little wrinkle in his brow. *He doesn't look happy,* Fleygur thought.

"Come on, son, it's not happening," he said abruptly, "Let's go home. Never heard anything so ridiculous. Four thousand pounds for an overgrown Shetland Pony, and a lame one at that!"

"He's not a pony, he's a horse," Roger

protested, "They only have Icelandic horses in Iceland. They're not ponies, they're...horses, Viking horses... not ponies." He trailed off.

Fleygur thought it sounded quite good, Viking Horses, what's not to like?

But Roger's dad didn't seem that impressed. He looked at Roger with a little smile. "Well, I am glad we got that straight!" He ruffled Roger's hair and glanced at Fleygur. "Sorry Rog, I am sure he's a very nice...*horse*, but we just can't afford him. Come on, best you stay away. That Jones is very unpredictable!"

As Roger's dad rested his hand on his son's back, gently steering him towards the gate, Roger looked back over his shoulder. His face looked soft and his mouth was turned down. Fleygur didn't like the way that made him feel. Something wasn't right, the boy couldn't be leaving him, not now. Fleygur nickered anxiously, *where are you going?*

Roger twisted free from his father's hand, and ran back to Fleygur. He stroked Fleygur's neck, pressing his forehead to Fleygur's, but he didn't speak.

"Come on!" The boy's father called from the car. Roger sighed as he turned away from Fleygur.

*People come and people go,* thought Fleygur, as he watched the boy climb the gate. *Like horses.*

Roger looked back at Fleygur one last time

from the gate, then opened the car door and got in.

*He's my only friend*, thought Fleygur. *I'm a herd of one without Roger.* He called to the boy, *don't go!* Fleygur starting trotting, then cantering towards the gate. *Wait for me!* he whinnied, as the car pulled away, but the boy was already gone.

Fleygur was alone again.

## CHAPTER 18
### Hercules the Shetland

Roger was grinning as he jumped the gate the next morning, and surprised Fleygur by running straight at him, throwing his arms around his neck. Fleygur flinched little, but he didn't move. This was Roger, and he trusted him.

"YOU...ARE...MINE!...MINE! I did it, I did it! Dad said 'no-way', you were too expensive... end-of...but Mum promised...before the accident, she promised I could have a horse of my own when I was ten, and I'm nearly twelve now. I told Dad she would have bought you for me...and he agreed! You are mine...MINE!"

Fleygur was confused by Roger's excitement and loud emotions, but when Roger slipped a halter on and led him out through the gate and onto the lane, he got a little excited too, and jogged. Something good was happening at last, something with this boy Roger.

"It's not far, we can walk it. Dad says I can't ride you until you've settled in."

Fleygur had never been out through this gate, or along this lane, but it felt good to be out of that field, and walking along with Roger. His ears flicked back and forth as he took in the unfamiliar places, but he never broke step with the boy, and after a while he dropped his head and tucked his nose in behind Roger's back, trusting where ever the boy wanted to take him.

Roger led him into a very small yard with four wooden stables, and as they approached a brown nose with a huge cream forelock appeared over the door of one of them. Fleygur hadn't realised there was a horse in there, and this one was so small that he had to stretch his neck up to get his nose over the door.

*Hello Shorty*, Fleygur nickered, happy to see another horse again. The nose promptly disappeared.

"That's Hercules," said Roger, tying Fleygur's rope to the metal ring next to the stable. "You two are going to be mates. Come on, Hercs, I've brought you a new friend, say hello to Fleygur."

Roger leant over the door and ruffled the pony's mane. "I've got treats!"

The brown nose re-appeared over the door and snuffled up the treat. Looking over at Fleygur from under his forelock, the pony put his ears back.

*That's Hercules to you*, snorted Hercules, as Roger disappeared toward the house. *Not Shorty, Fluffy, Titch or Stumpy...Hercules. I've been round* here a long time and taught that boy everything about horses, so don't you go messing things up.

Am I your replacement? Fleygur asked.

Don't be ridiculous, snorted Hercules, you don't replace a Shetland pony, you add to them. One Shetland pony is good, but two is better, and if you have two you might as well have three or four, or more. At least that's what my mistress Anna used to say.

Where is your mistress? Fleygur asked.

Gone, said Hercules.

Gone where? Fleygur asked.

Just gone. I use to have a big herd. Four Shetlands and Welsh Cob called Bess. Bess was always coming back from Shows, prancing around and flaunting her rosettes. I had to remind her that I was the first. I taught my mistress Anna to ride, and the boy, when he was big enough. My Anna was here everyday, then one day she didn't come. Tom came and let us out into the field, and then he went again. When he came back he just sat in the field with us, very quiet. We gathered around him, standing with our heads low. I put my nose into his hands and nuzzled him. Then the boy came too, and buried his face in my mane and cried. I knew then that my mistress Anna was not coming back, not ever.

How did you know? asked Fleygur.

You don't get to be thirty-five years old without learning a thing or two about humans, Hercules replied.

Fleygur looked at the other stables but he

couldn't feel or smell any other horses. *Where are the other horses?* he asked.

*Tom said they couldn't keep us all, now our mistress was gone. I was allowed to stay, because he trusted me to look after the boy.*

Both the horses looked round as Roger reappeared, with his father in tow, still grinning and beaming happy feelings.

The boy's father smiled. "Well, I hope you are happy now," he said. "He certainly looks happy to be here. I think it'll be okay to turn them out in the field together, but you are going to have to restrict the grass, even I can see that horse is dangerously overweight."

"I'll get him fit, said Roger, "It's half-term soon, and then it's not long to the summer holidays. I'll be able to ride every day."

"Okay, but no riding, unless I am home, or Joan is keeping an eye, that's the deal." There was a pause "Okay?"

"Sure," replied Roger, but Fleygur didn't think that Roger was really paying attention, he was gazing out of the yard and up to the nearby hills.

It had only taken one of Roger's visits with a carrot in the morning, for Fleygur to consider it a well established ritual. So when he heard a door open he was already quick marching towards the gate by the time Roger appeared around the side of the stables. His nose vibrated with a quiet nicker of welcome. Fleygur snuffled the carrot from Roger's hand, feeling the explosion of cold sweetness in his mouth as he listened to Roger whispering something about their first ride, *very soon.*

"Don't be late for school," the boy's father called from the front porch of the house.

"Okay, I'm going now."

Fleygur watched Roger leave the yard on his bike and turned back to munching grass. Roger would be gone for several hours, plenty of time for eating.

A short while later Roger's father crossed the yard on his way to his big black car. Fleygur lifted his head, hopeful of another treat, but the boy's father was already opening the car door. Then he glanced across at Fleygur and paused.

"I really hope this is a good idea," he said to himself, and then looking Fleygur right in the eyes he said, "You'd better take care of my boy, he's all I have now."

He got in, started the engine, and drove out of the yard.

*That boy spoils you,* said Hercules. *All those carrots are not good for you, you know.*

Fleygur flicked his tail at the horseflies and ignored Hercules. *The grass is much more interesting than a know-it-all Shetland pony,* thought Fleygur.

He'd been at Roger's home for nearly a week. He knew the best breezy spot on top of the hill for a mid-morning doze; the best oak tree for shade when the sun was high, and he knew that the occasional bang of the bird-scarers from the farmer's field next door was nothing to worry about. Right now he was concentrating on finding the best bits of grazing, strategically turning his bum towards Hercules to discourage him from encroaching on HIS grass. It wasn't working. Hercules just barged right on in with his ears back.

*Budge over, you,* said Hercules, *I want some of that.*

Fleygur tried to hold his ground. He leant into Hercules, trying to bite his lower leg to move him, but Hercules whipped around and aimed his two back feet in Fleygur's direction. *Take that!*

Fleygur jumped out of the way. Hercules wasn't really going to hurt him, but Fleygur knew when the boss-horse was laying down the law, and decided to let him have his way.

All of a sudden Fleygur heard footsteps just behind him. He whipped up his head, his muscles tensed, ready to run, but as he caught sight of Roger the adrenaline rush drained away and he nickered a greeting instead.

"Hello Fleygur!" Roger said, "Surprised you, did I? I was hiding round the corner 'til Dad left. We're not waiting any longer!"

## CHAPTER 19
### Roger's First Ride

Trickles of excitement leaked from all over the boy as he gave Fleygur a quick rub on the forehead and slipped on his bridle. Fleygur flicked his ears and turned his head to watch Roger as he lifted on the saddle, checked the girth and finally the fit of the bridle, sliding two fingers under the noseband, just as Philippa used to do. The boy's gentleness and little scratches and rubs were hypnotic. Fleygur dropped his head and ambled after Roger to the mounting block.

"Anyone would think you were a crazy horse, the way Dad's been going on," mumbled Roger as he stepped up on the block. Fleygur stood absolutely still.

"That Jones is the crazy one," continued Roger, picking up the reins. "Everyone knows he's rubbish with horses, just 'coz he got all that money from his Grandad, shouldn't give him the right to own horses. He's a first class idiot!" Announced Roger as he swung into the saddle.

The boy was so much lighter than Jones that at first Fleygur could barely tell he was there.

He could feel Roger's hands on the end of the reins, but there was no pressure on his mouth. As Fleygur waited, the excitement seeped slowly from Roger's body and into his. Fleygur's heart rate quickened.

"We'll be fine, won't we boy?" said Roger, sounding slightly less confident now he was in the saddle.

Fleygur pricked his ears. He was ready and his muscles trembled, anticipating the signal for go. Roger's legs lightly brushed his sides and Fleygur shot forward, ready to race off in fast tölt.

"Whoa," said Roger, losing his balance and tipping back in the saddle, "Easy, boy," his voice wobbled slightly. Fleygur dropped out of tölt and back to walk, his very fast walk. *I can walk, if that's what the boy wants.*

"Wow!" said Roger, as Fleygur marched out through the gate onto the bridleway. "That's some speedy walk!"

The morning sunshine was warm on his glossy black coat, and his double-sided mane was flapping with the rhythm of his hoof-steps. Fleygur just knew they looked awesome. He didn't need to know where they were going, Roger knew and that was good enough for him. As they rode down the track alongside the field Hercules whinnied a goodbye.

*See you later, Shorty!* Fleygur whickered back,

knowing he was too far away to get kicked for his rudeness, but as Fleygur lost sight of Hercules behind the trees he hesitated, slowing his walk. Anxiety prickled through this body and he snorted. He didn't really want to leave his new friend. Roger leant forward and gave him a scratch, squeezing him with his legs and feeling reassured, Fleygur quickened his pace again.

They left the track and crossed a narrow lane, near the entrance to a big house, and started down a long wide bridleway lined with trees. Fleygur had been here before, with Jones, when he use to run for home. He started jogging and felt Roger's hands tighten slightly on the reins.

"Okay," said Roger, "let's try this tölt thingy."

Fleygur felt tension increase in Roger's body and he was off, his feet making a tick-a-tack-er-tick-er-tack-er beat on the hard mud. He knew Roger had one of those wrinkly happy faces.

"WOW," Roger said, "So powerful! You're the one that should be called Hercules!"

Tick-er-tack-er-tick-er-tack-er, Fleygur was picking up speed, the adrenaline pumping harder around his body. His excitement began to bubble over as the instinct to run started to possess him. *Time to get back to Hercules,* he thought.

"Easy boy," said Roger.

Tick-er-tack-er-tick-er-tack-er...

"Easy, boy!"

Fleygur felt the reins tightened in his mouth and he gripped the bit with his teeth. He remembered Jones on his back, and the pain. *Faster*, thought Fleygur, *faster*, as he felt panic growing in him.

"Whoa!" Roger's voice was sounding more urgent now. The pull on the reins jammed the unforgiving hard metal bit against the fleshy parts of Fleygur's jaw. Fleygur stuck his nose in the air and shook his head to loosen it, but as he did the saddle tipped, pressing on the sore part of his back. He shot forward into a flat out gallop. His instinct was in full control and it said, *Run Fleygur Run!* He couldn't hear Roger's shouts anymore, just the thunder of his hoof-beats getting faster and faster. As he rounded a corner of the bridleway Fleygur felt the weight in the saddle lurch to one side and the reins go slack. He stumbled and slowed to regain his footing. Small hands were grabbing at his mane, and then he heard Roger's voice saying, "Whoa, boy, whoa!"

*Roger?* He could feel the boy bouncing in the saddle and the metal stirrups banging on his sides. *Something's wrong!* He slid to a stop, and Roger sailed over his head landing face first on the dirt in front of him. The boy didn't move.

Fleygur's pulse slowed as his flight instinct quickly ebbed away. He stepped carefully towards the boy and nuzzled the back of Roger's hair with his lips.

*What you doing down there?* he snorted.

Roger groaned, and slowly rolled over until he was lying flat on his back, looking up Fleygur's nostrils. The boy's face looked different. It wasn't wrinkly now, it was covered in dirt, and a trickle of blood was running down his forehead and into his left eye.

Fleygur didn't know what to do so he breathed out on Roger's face,

*You're not supposed to be down there.*

Roger wiped his right arm over his bloodied face, and reaching for Fleygur's mane he hauled himself to his feet.

"We're going to have to work on your brakes," he said, his voice a little weak. He turned, and limping slightly, led Fleygur towards home.

Dust flew from Fleygur's coat, as he shook after his roll, creating a cloud around him before it drifted off in the breeze. Roger watched him from the gate, the blood crusting on his forehead. The boy turned as his father's car pulled into the yard.

"Uh-oh. Now I'm for it!" he said.

Fleygur bobbed his head, picking up the anxiety that suddenly flowed from the boy.

"The School rang...," began his father, in a clipped voice, but as Roger turned to faced him, he stopped, his brow creasing. "What have you

138

done to your face?"

Roger lifted his hand to his forehead.

"Oh...er...I had a fight...on the way to school."

His father raised his eyebrows.

"I...I...er, this boy...he...called me names," Roger blurted out.

The boy's father waited. His face fixed. "Go on," he said.

"He asked where my 'girly pony' was...and pushed me...so I hit him."

"And...?" asked his father, not sounding at all convinced.

Fleygur wondered when the boy would get to the bit about him face-planting in the dirt after the emergency stop.

"I...er...he...pushed me over and I banged my head" Roger continued, stumbling over his words.

"What's the boy's name?" demanded his father. Fleygur twitched his ears, the man's voice sounded cross.

"I dunno. Maybe he's in another year, or another school...or he's new," Roger said quickly.

Roger's dad kept a steady gaze on his son's face. The boy shifted his weight from one foot to the other and looked at the floor. "I...I...my head was bleeding, so I came home," he mumbled.

Roger's father looked across at Fleygur, and

the boy followed his gaze. Fleygur curled his top lip and did an enormous yawn, as the remaining excitement from the morning's ride drained away. Roger gave him lopsided grin, but quickly went back to serious-face when his father looked back at him.

"You've not been riding that horse then?" Roger's father said, giving his son a long hard stare.

"No Dad. I was going to school, honest. Those boys keep picking on me...and most of girls only want to be friends 'coz I've got a horse, except Rowan, I think she actually likes me."

His father stayed silent. Roger shuffled his feet, kicking at the dirt.

"It's hard. School. All the writing and..." Roger's eyes filled with tears, and one trickled down the boy's cheek. His dad's eyes softened a little.

Fleygur stretched his neck over the fence and huffed into the back of Roger's neck. The boy let out a small choked laugh and turned to hug him, wiping his tears in Fleygur's mane.

"Come on. Let's get you cleaned up. I'll drop you at school," his father said, putting his arm around Roger. "I have the same difficulty as you, with writing and stuff, but it didn't stop me becoming a nurse now, did it?"

"No Dad," Roger sighed, and looked at his feet again.

"You're not stupid, just dyslexic. I'll talk to your teacher, but you can't keep missing school. I can't be called away from work all the time. I've already changed my shifts, you know money is tight."

Roger's shoulders slumped as his father led him back to the house.

Fleygur watched until the front door closed, hoping for a last minute treat. Then wandered off to hassle Hercules, biting behind his knees to try to get him to play, but Hercules was having none of it today. *I'm stiff, I am thirty-five you know! Besides, you dropped my boy. Good riding horses don't do that*, Hercules said grumpily, putting his ears back and waving his nose at Fleygur.

*He's my boy now*, thought Fleygur, but he didn't say so. Hercules was in a bad mood, so it was best to stay out of his way.

## CHAPTER 20
### Bullies and Dogs

At the weekend Roger practically bounced out of the house and ran across the yard, Fleygur's halter jingling on his arm. *You're going somewhere,* said Hercules, delicately plucking a purple thistle flower with his lips.

"Dad says I can ride today!" Roger called out, eyes sparkling and a huge grin.

*Told you so,* said Hercules, his mouth now stuffed with the juicy thistle stalk. He pulled funny faces as he tried to eat it without spiking his mouth on the prickles.

"You're such a goof, Hercs." Roger laughed.

Fleygur meandered over to the boy and frisked his pockets, expertly identifying the one with the treats, and tugging at the pocket flap with his teeth.

"Later!" laughed Roger, brushing Fleygur's nose away, "Work to do first." He slipped Fleygur's halter on. "I have to show Dad that I can look after you AND go to school. I don't think he believed me about the fight, and I'm in deep trouble for bunking off already."

Tacked up and ready to go Fleygur stood in the middle of the yard, next to Roger. Roger kicked at the dirt with his boots and kept looking up at the house. Fleygur didn't waste energy fidgeting, he just waited, motionless.

Finally Roger's father appeared from the house. "Okay, let's see it," he said.

Roger put one foot in the stirrup and hopped on. Leaning forward he whispered to Fleygur, "Keep calm this time. Don't want to scare him!"

Roger pointed Fleygur towards the field gate.

*I know this one,* thought Fleygur, swinging his back end around and side-stepping so he was lined up parallel to the gate.

"See! Told you he was clever, he knew just what to do!" said Roger, flashing a grin at his dad. Fleygur waited as Roger leant forward and unhooked the latch, then a little squeeze from the boy's leg told Fleygur he was ready. Carefully Fleygur stepped backwards and to the side as Roger held onto the gate with one hand. Together they turned around the end of the gate, and Fleygur side-stepped again until he heard the latch click closed.

"Good boy," said Roger, giving Fleygur a scratch just in front of his saddle.

"Very impressive," said the boy's father.

They rode around the edge of the field three times. Fleygur could feel the calm heart-beat of the boy and, following the rhythm of his breathing, he took long relaxed strides as he walked. Hercules was grazing in the middle of the field, occasionally following Fleygur's progress with his head. Fleygur looked smart, he knew he did, arching his neck just so. He was a horse of the Vikings, and it wasn't all charging about with his mane flying, he could do elegant and noble too.

Roger glanced at his dad. "Now we're going to tölt," he said. Gradually Roger asked Fleygur for a quicker and quicker walk, and feeling the change in the boy's body, Fleygur stepped up to a slow tölt, lifting his front legs high, Roger sitting steady on his back.

"That's pretty impressive too," said the boy's father, "How did you learn that?"

"Fleygur just knows, it's his favourite gait... and I watched one of Jones's lessons," said Roger.

"Well, he does look good," said his dad "I guess you can take him out for a ride then. Just a short one, to see how you do. You got your phone charged up?"

"Yes. Come on, Fleygur!" Roger sounded really excited.

"Just round the bridleway loop, I don't want you riding on the roads on your own. No galloping either. Understand?"

"Yes, Dad!"

Roger's dad smiled at his son as he opened the gate, "I wish your mum was here to see this."

Fleygur felt the boy tense and his breathing stop for a moment. Then the muscles in his body went slack, as if something had drained the joy from him. The change unsettled Fleygur. He nickered anxiously to Hercules, but he was busy eating nettles and didn't reply.

"Me too," Roger said quietly as he urged Fleygur through the gate and onto the track that went up the hill behind the house.

As they rode up the rough track into the shade of the steep banks, Fleygur could tell that Roger was smiling again. The lane became stoney and as they squeezed between two high hedges Fleygur caught sight of a shadow moving ahead of them. Still feeling worried about leaving Hercules he jerked his head up and swivelled his ears forwards.

"It's okay, Fleygur," Roger said, "it's just someone on a bike...oh, no!"

Fleygur felt Roger stiffen.

"It's Jess," he whispered.

Fleygur pranced a little. The boy was nervous. *Should he run?*

A girl with spiky blond hair, wearing pale blue ripped jeans, was bouncing along over the stones towards them on a brightly painted mountain bike. A broad grin spread across her face as she jammed on the breaks, sliding the rear wheel around and sending a shower of small stones towards them. Fleygur snorted.

"Look who it is," she drawled, sarcasm dripping from her mouth. "Is this your fluffy-wuffy pony then? Oh My God, look how fat he is!!"

"Let us pass," Roger said, squeezing Fleygur's sides. As Fleygur stepped forward he saw Jess's eyes widen in alarm as she hastily stepped off the bike and held it between them.

"Make me!" she said, trying to make herself look tall.

Fleygur wasn't fooled, he could feel her fear from six feet away, but Roger didn't seem to notice. Fleygur sensed the boy's uncertainty, and his desire to get going, so he stamped his front foot and advanced towards the girl. Jess quickly dragged the bike to one side and pressed herself back against the hedge as they squeezed past.

"Look at the belly on that!" she shouted from behind, "Haha, Woger's got a roly-poly pony!"

As they left Jess behind, still laughing and shouting after them, Roger breathed out again and relaxed. Fleygur lowered his head and breathed out too. At the end of the bridleway there was a small tarmac lane heading towards the village, or a long straight bridleway leading towards home, and to the right a small lane with a sign saying

'Private Road.' They turned right into the private road and past a couple of cottages.

"That doesn't count as riding on a road," Roger said under his breath.

Fleygur kept to a nice steady walk, hoping they weren't going too far from home. He'd got used to being with Hercules now and was worried about being away from him.

"Come on, boy, no dawdling," Roger said, squeezing with his legs. "Now we just have to get past Stealth Dog. Don't be scared, she can't get you."

But Fleygur could feel Roger tense up and he jogged a little. Dogs are loud and can usually be heard a mile off. He could smell dog everywhere, but he couldn't see or hear one. Maybe there was no dog here at all. They passed into a narrow gap between two brown beech hedges, and the boy's hands tightened on the reins. "Easy, boy," said Roger. Fleygur couldn't sense any danger, but the boy clearly thought there was some, so he tensed up, ready to run. Halfway along the narrow passage Fleygur could see the bridleway opening out ahead of them. The boy let out the breath he had been holding. "Phew. Maybe she's not home today..."

Then, suddenly the hedge came alive, "Wuff-wuff-wuff-grr-grr-woof!"

Fleygur tucked his back legs under and

whipped around to see a small black bundle of fur with white teeth hurtling itself at the hedge. Fleygur tried to side step, but the path was too narrow.

*Come here and I'll stamp on you!* He snorted. The hysterical dog just barked and snarled more ferociously.

"Easy," said Roger, "she can't get you."

The dog abruptly broke off her surprise attack as they cleared the end of the hedges, and gambolled back down the garden, her tongue lolling out of her mouth, looking very pleased with herself.

Fleygur jogged a little, trying to look behind him to check that the dog was not about to leap at him again.

"I hate that dog," muttered Roger. Fleygur decided he didn't like her much either.

The bridleway was in a deep cutting lined with trees, and sloped slightly uphill. Fleygur could smell the recent presence of other horses and snorted a little in excitement. Maybe he could catch them up! As they rounded the corner Roger urged him into a canter, leaning forward.

"Don't tell Dad," he laughed as they bombed up the hill, weaving between the trees.

Fleygur ran out of puff before they reached the top of the hill, and though he could have run forever if Stealth Dog had been chasing him, it was much harder running just for fun, without fear to provide the extra boost. He was happy to slow to a walk as they reached the end of the bridleway, and turned onto a narrow track that looped back through the trees to their field.

Roger's father was waiting for them at the gate, relief spreading over his face as Fleygur marched up to him, whinnying to Hercules, *I'm back!*

*Heard you a mile away,* said Hercules.

"How was it?" Roger's father asked.

"Brilliant!" said Roger, swinging his right leg over Fleygur's head and jumping off. "He was ace!"

## CHAPTER 21
### Something is Wrong

A light breeze whipped up the leaves as Fleygur and Roger set off the next day. Fleygur's ears worked overtime, trying to work out if it was just the bushes being slapped about by the wind, or a horse-eating monster out to get him. Being front-horse and back-horse meant he had to keep an eye on everything, and he wished Hercules was with him to help with look-out duties. Fleygur was ready for Stealth Dog's antics this time though, so when she launched her attack he didn't run, but still her yapping and snarling pricked his deep instinct, passed on from mother to foal for generations. *Wolf,* it told him, *run run!'*

"Easy," Roger said, as Fleygur jogged a little, fighting the urge to flee. "It's just that stupid dog."

When Roger turned him left at the fork in the bridleway Fleygur immediately knew where this path led, even though he had not been on it before. Instinctively he knew it was the way home, back to Hercules.

Fleygur jogged.

Roger tightened the reins.

"Easy, boy," he said.

Fleygur slowed, trying hard to do what Roger wanted, but it was difficult to concentrate on the boy, when all he could think about was getting home. Fleygur quickened his pace again.

"Steady, boy." Roger tightened the rein.

*Why can't we just go?* Fleygur thought, and he started to run.

"Whoa!" Roger said, squeezing his thighs and pushing down with his seat bones. Fleygur felt the signal through the saddle and stopped dead. He shook his nose about in frustration. He waited for a moment, but the excitement of getting back to Hercules was too much for him to contain and he started forward.

"No!" Roger raised his voice and pulled hard on the reins. Fleygur tossed his head and stamped. *Why stop? Let's go home!*

"We are going to stand here until you calm down," Roger said, "I decide when we go, not you!" He was starting to sound cross.

Fleygur stood still, as his will to please the boy battled with his urge to get home. After a moment his *home* urge won, and he started forward again.

"NO!" Roger shouted this time, and gave a sharp pull on the rein. The bit banged onto Fleygur's jaw.

Fleygur was annoyed at the pain in his mouth. He stuck his nose out and pulled back, and went forward several steps gradually speeding up. Roger shortened one rein and pulled Fleygur's head around.

"You are NOT bolting for home," he said, a small shake in his voice giving away his fear.

Fleygur went round in a tight circle, until finally he submitted to the boy and stopped.

*This is unfair,* thought Fleygur, tossing his head, his eyeballs rolling inside their sockets, showing white flashes that were usually hidden behind his big brown eyes. Now it was his turn to be cross. Cross with this boy who wouldn't let him get back to his herd. Fleygur looked wild and now his temper rose to match it. He could sense Roger's tense muscles and rapid breathing that told him the boy was afraid.

*What was frightening the boy?* Fleygur snorted nervously and shook his head against the restraining reins.

As he waited for the signal to go Fleygur's heart pumped faster. The urge to run was getting stronger. His legs trembled with anticipation. Finally Roger released the rein, and squeezed his lower legs. Fleygur sprang forward, the pent up energy released in one blast. He wasn't thinking about what gait or speed the boy had asked for, all he could think about was getting home, where he would feel safe. His hooves drummed on the dry earth, and branches whipped past his head at such speed that he didn't even notice as some bashed into his face and clawed at his mane. He ignored the yelps from Roger as they blasted though the low branches. He was going home, that is all there was to it.

Suddenly, the bit was pulled part way through his mouth, only stopped by the metal side bar that now pressed on the right side of his face, forcing his head around. Fleygur shook his head from side to side, trying to release the pressure. He tried to keep running but as he was twisted around he started to miss his footing.

"NO, NO!" yelled Roger. Fleygur stumbled to a stop, facing away from home. Fleygur could hear the anger in the Roger's voice, but he was not just angry, he was scared-angry, and that was the worst type. Scared-anger was out of control, unpredictable, like Jones. Fleygur was blowing hard through his nostrils and flinging his head up and down.

"You can NOT RUN HOME," Roger shouted. Then he jabbed his heels into Fleygur's sides, his voice deeper and rasped, as he shouted again, "Right! You want to gallop? You can gallop this way!"

Fleygur was confused. *What now?* He didn't understand this lesson. *Did the boy want him to run home or stop still? Why was he pulling on his mouth and kicking? Why was he hurting him?*

Fleygur hesitated.

"Go on, GALLOP" shouted Roger again, urging him with his body. So Fleygur ran, but not as fast as before because he was heading away from home. Roger pulled him up again, and turned him back towards home.

"Now WALK," he said. But Fleygur's mind was still in 'run' mode. He wanted more than ever to get home as fast as possible, away from this confusion and away from this boy! He launched straight into gallop. It made sense to Fleygur, but obviously not to Roger, who hauled on the reins yelling, "NO….WALK!"

Fleygur, his head pulled around by the rein, stumbled to a halt again. Roger turned him away from home again and shouted, "GO," jabbing at Fleygur's sides with his heels.

Fleygur was breathing hard and the insides of his nostrils were bright red as the blood pumped through his veins. Small lines of sweat trickled down his chest and the backs of his legs. This explosion from Roger didn't make sense. He was only doing what had worked in the past. When Jones said 'go,' Fleygur galloped as fast as he could for home.

*Maybe this boy was just like Jones after all,* he thought. The gentle kindness of Philippa was a very distant memory now. Maybe this was what being a riding horse was like, with a pain in his back, a sore mouth, and humans who didn't listen. When the boy had rescued him from Jones, Fleygur thought he could trust him, but now he was shouting, jabbing at him, pulling on him, confusing him. Hurting him! Anger swirled in Fleygur's mind calling on his body to fight. He fought to get his head down low so he could pivot on his front legs and buck the boy off, but Roger held the reins firmly and pushed him forwards; then he turned him sharply again. As they stopped Fleygur snorted, waiting for the next jab or the kick. But Roger didn't move. Fleygur lifted his head and took a few tentative steps forward, uncertain if this was what the boy wanted.

"Whoa," said Roger, but quietly this time. Fleygur felt a squeeze from the boys thighs and stopped.

*What now?* He stomped a foot. Adrenaline was still surging in Fleygur's body. His mind was fuzzy and the sounds around him grew until he could hardly bear it. If he couldn't move soon he would explode.

Then, just at the moment Fleygur felt he could hold himself no longer, the boy let out a huge long breath, as if he had been holding it this whole time. Fleygur felt Roger's tension release, and almost without thinking he lowered his head and snorted away some of his own tension too. Then Roger's body begin to shake, and Fleygur

155

heard a soft sob. He flicked his ears back to listen to the boy. This was new, *what did it mean? Is the boy sick?*

"I'm sorry, Fleygur," Roger said, leaning forward and wrapping his arms around Fleygur's neck. "I lost my temper."

Roger slid from Fleygur's back and stood in front of him. Fleygur felt better now he could see the boy. Roger wiped some tears from his face. "Maybe I can't do this after all," he said, "Mum said you should never lose your temper with a horse. Mum said…" his voice choked up as more tears leaked from his eyes and trickled down his cheeks. "I'm sorry," he whispered.

*He's not like Jones after all,* thought Fleygur, his own energy dropping to meet Roger's. *He's just a boy, a young colt whose still learning.* Fleygur reached out with his nose and nuzzled Roger's hands with his lips. Roger smiled.

"You are not a bad horse, I know you are not," he said.

*I know that too,* thought Fleygur, and snuffle-snorted in the boy's face. Roger laughed in spite of his tears.

"Something's not right," Roger said finally. "Something is wrong…and I am going to figure out what it is!" he announced, drawing himself up and taking hold of Fleygur's reins.

*Well about time,* thought Fleygur. Lifting his

head he pointed his ears at Roger in expectation. Roger looked directly into Fleygur's eyes. "We're going to start from the beginning," he said, "You and me."

Fleygur liked the calm boy much better than the angry one. It made him want to be with him. He tucked his head in behind Roger, his nose practically touching the boy's back, as they turned and walked for home.

## CHAPTER 22
**Starting Again**

As the moon dropped below the horizon giving way to a warm summer sun, Fleygur and Hercules were already standing at the gate, waiting for their morning treat. It was not a school day. Fleygur knew when it was not, as movement in the human house started later than usual. This particular morning Roger burst from the house and ran towards the horses, carrying a tangled pile of rope. His eyes danced with excitement as he announced, "It's Half Term, half way to the Summer Holidays! Today we are going back to the beginning Fleygur, with Ground Work."

Hercules snorted. *You're going to be busy. When humans have holidays, horses work more!*

Hercules pawed the ground to remind Roger that he had not handed out any treats yet. Fleygur nodded his head and licked his lips in support of Hercules's demand for food, but Roger had dropped the tangled rope on the ground and, having found one loose end, he was intent on untangling the rest.

"Ah ha!" said Roger at last, looking up with a

satisfied expression as he slung the neatly coiled rope over his shoulder. "Oh, sorry guys...," he fumbled in his pocket. "Here you go," he said, holding one hand out to each horse. It didn't matter to Fleygur that the carrots were a bit old, a bit soft and coated in dust from the boy's pockets. Treats were treats, and sweet carrots were his favourites.

As the horses munched, Roger climbed over the fence and slipped a loop of the rope over Fleygur's nose, and then another loop over his ears.

"There! That's a training halter," he said, standing back and looking very pleased with himself. "I found it in Mum's box."

Fleygur turned his head to look at the boy, and the looped rope promptly fell off his nose and hung loosely below his chin.

"Mm...it's a bit big," Roger said, fiddling with the knots. He slipped the tighter loop back over Fleygur's nose and made a few more adjustments, before taking up the end of the rope and heading towards the gate.

Fleygur followed, but as each step took him further away from Hercules his anxiety increased. He didn't like leaving his herd-mate. He had been friends with Blossi and he'd left, and the time had come when he had to leave his mother, brother and best friend, Gydja. He had made friends with Jinks, Lina and Ginger, and even the big Cob, Beanie, but he had to leave them too. As they headed towards the gate Fleygur slowed, the slack in the rope slowly tightening. Roger didn't notice until Fleygur stopped completely and the rope went tight between them. Roger gave a little pull. As the rope halter tightened around Fleygur's face, he took another step forward to ease the pressure and stopped again. Roger was calm and happy today, but Fleygur remembered the last time they went out. The boy was angry and shouting. Fleygur's back was sore, his mouth had hurt and the boy had hurt him more. He had been in the field a whole week, hanging out with Hercules, eating, sleeping, rolling. He didn't want to be shouted at again, and he didn't want to leave Hercules. Roger turned to look at him.

"What's up, Fleygur?"

Tension trickled though Fleygur's face, and as his muscles tensed deep wrinkles appeared on the end of his nose.

"Come ON..." Roger said, taking up slack in the rope, but then he stopped. "No," he said, "I promised, we are starting from scratch. I have to know what's wrong."

He looked at Fleygur, properly looked at him.

Fleygur's eyes narrowed as he looked back at the boy, trying really hard to tell him about his fear and his pain. Roger's eyes flicked towards

Fleygur's nose and his own eyebrows wrinkled together in a puzzled expression.

"What's up?" he said, "You usually just come."

Roger gave another pull on the rope and Fleygur took a reluctant step forward, but his ears were pointing backwards, towards where Hercules was munching happily on the grass.

Roger studied Fleygur's face really hard, and then, finally, his gaze followed the direction of Fleygur's ears. The wrinkles in his brow released as his eyes widened slightly in a moment of recognition.

"Ah!" he said, "You don't want to leave Hercs! Is that it? Is that why you rush home too?" Roger said, seemingly pleased with his deduction. He stepped in close to Fleygur and gave him a reassuring scratch under his mane. "It's okay Fleygur, we're just going in the schooling area, you'll be able to see Hercs the whole time."

Hercules lifted his head at the sound of his name and nickered, *treats?* Getting no response, he went back to his grazing. Fleygur was enjoying the scratches from Roger, and the sound of his calm voice was reassuring. Roger slipped a hand in his pocket and held out a piece of carrot a few feet in front of Fleygur, and made a cluck sound, pulling gently on the rope. Fleygur stepped forward and took the carrot.

"Good fella," said Roger rubbing Fleygur's

neck. "Now, let's go and you can have more of those."

Chewing on the carrot made Fleygur feel better. This time when Roger walked on Fleygur tucked his head in behind Roger and followed.

*Humans are such hard work,* thought Fleygur. *Horses have to practically shout their signals before humans notice them. This boy is clever though. He can horse-talk, if only he remembers to pay attention.*

Now that Fleygur knew their training sessions were fun and involved treats, he happily followed Roger through the gate the next morning. Watching Roger's body movements Fleygur learnt to anticipate exactly what he wanted. When the boy changed the hand that was holding the rope, Fleygur spun around and circled him in the other direction. When Roger went very still and brought his hands together Fleygur stopped, and flicked his ears towards the boy to show that he was still paying attention. The quicker Fleygur responded to Roger's movements the bigger the grin on the boy's face.

Fleygur had just changed direction for the second time when a movement caught his attention and looked towards the yard. Roger followed his gaze.

## CHAPTER 23
### Rowan

A small girl was standing on the bottom rung of the yard gate, watching them. Her long red hair tumbled over her shoulders, and she had such a huge smile that she looked like she was all bright white teeth and shinning eyes.

"That's a-ma-zing, Rog!" she called. "Your pony's so cute. Can I stroke him?"

Fleygur halted as Roger closed his hands together.

"Sure, come on," he said.

The girl let out a little squeal as she clambered over the gate and ran across the yard.

"You have to be quiet around horses, Rowan," Roger said, in his serious voice, "and don't run, you'll scare him."

Rowan's bright smile fleetingly vanished as she abruptly slowed to walk.

"Oh, sorry, I wouldn't want to do that," she said. "He's so cute, I didn't know you had a new pony, oh wow, look at that crescent moon on his face, and all that hair. What's his name? Are you going to ride him soon?"

163

"He's called Flay-gur. It's Icelandic, it means the Flying One. He's an Icelandic horse, not a pony," Roger said.

Fleygur was enjoying being the centre of attention, and the excuse for a rest from going round in circles. He lowered his head, allowing the girl to stroke his neck.

"Oh, he's lov-er-ly!" cooed Rowan. "How did you get him all the way from Iceland? My dad's been to Iceland. He said it was amazing! Did your pony come in a plane? Imagine that, a pony in a plane!"

"He's a horse," Roger said sternly. "And he was born in England. It says so in his passport. His mum was born in Iceland though. So he's a proper Icelandic horse."

"Horses have passports?" Rowan giggled, "Do they have those little square photos too?"

"Don't be silly," Roger chuckled. "How would you get a horse in one of those booths!" They both burst into laughter.

Fleygur didn't understand what they were talking about, but he liked it when Roger was happy, and nuzzled at his hands for another scratch. Fleygur flicked his ears towards the road as a blue van pulled up in their gateway. Roger turned to look, and the van pulled off again, one wheel spinning on the loose stones.

"Who was that?" Rowan asked.

"Dunno," Roger said, "not seen that van before."

Rowan shrugged her shoulders, "Anyway, got to go. Thanks for letting me say hello to your pony." She puckered her lips and pressed them on to Fleygur's nose, making a funny squeaking sound, before crossing the yard and climbing back over the gate.

After Rowan had left Roger slipped the rope halter off. Fleygur tried to rub his sweaty ears on Roger, but Roger wasn't finished yet. Suddenly he dashed away laughing. Fleygur squealed, and cantered after him. Roger tried to dodge away from him, but Fleygur was right on it, matching him step for step. It felt good to be free of the bridle and all the ropes, and to run with his friend, just like they had done when Roger had found him in the grassy lane field, lame, abandoned and lonely.

On the third day of training, as Fleygur was circling around the boy, Roger's grin slowly faded. He watched Fleygur carefully as he asked for a change of direction several times. Fleygur began to get very warm, with all the switching around. Roger changed hands again and Fleygur spun around to the right-handed circle. This was harder for him than the left. His shoulder was a little stiff, and the small circles around the boy were more difficult. He liked the games without ropes better, where he was free to take bigger circles. When Roger brought his hands together Fleygur was glad to stop. Roger had a serious expression as he approached.

"You're stiff," he said, resting a hand on Fleygur's right shoulder. Roger worked his way down Fleygur's shoulder pressing lightly, then more firmly and as he did so Fleygur stepped away from the discomfort.

"Right, that's it. I am checking everything," said Roger. Slipping the rope halter from Fleygur's head and leaving him in the school, Roger disappeared into the house.

Fleygur stood for a moment, wondering where the boy had gone, and then feeling the soreness, and the itchiness from his sweaty coat, he dropped down for a roll, twisting and wriggling, then lying flat on one side to rub his face in the dirt. He was just scrambling back to his feet when Roger returned, clutching a battered cream and red hard-back book.

"The TV Vet Book," he read from the cover. "It was Mum's." Roger flicked through the pages. "It's very old, but there's something in here about examining horses...ah, here!" Roger climbed up on the gate and sat reading.

Fleygur watched for a moment, snuffled at Roger's feet, and then wandered off to scout the edges of the school for tasty plants, stopping now and again to scratch his itchy nose on a fence post.

Finally Roger snapped the book shut and jumped down from the gate. Fleygur stopped his food hunt and pricked his ears as the boy approached with a very determined look on his face. Roger ran his hands all over Fleygur's legs and shoulders, then he moved down his back pressing lightly on the muscles either side of his spine. Fleygur stood very still, but as Roger pressed on the sore part of his back he dipped his back away from the pain and side-stepped.

"That's right where your saddle goes!" said Roger, his voice rising in alarm. He put his hands on Fleygur's back again and pressed lightly, watching for Fleygur's reaction carefully. Fleygur didn't move this time. The gentle pressure was uncomfortable. It didn't really hurt, not that much, but he flicked his ears back and his nostrils tightened at the discomfort.

"Oh Fleygur!" breathed Roger, coming around to stand in front of him. Taking his nose between his two hands Roger lowered his forehead onto Fleygur's, and let out a huge sigh. "Right, last bit, I need to check your mouth." Roger slipped a thumb though the side of Fleygur's jaw, and with his hand over the top of his nose, gently pulled Fleygur's mouth open, bending to peer inside. Fleygur heard a sharp intake of breath. The boy released his mouth, his hands dropping to his sides. "Oh Fleygur, that bruise looks sore! How could I have not noticed!" Roger wrapped his arms around Fleygur's neck. "I am so sorry," he said, his voice muffled in Fleygur's thick mane. "Right," Roger said, "definitely no more riding until you are fixed. I am going to do it all from the ground until that bruise in your mouth is gone, and your back is better!"

## CHAPTER 24
### The Horse Has to Go!

A few weeks later and Fleygur was feeling a lot better. His back was no longer sore and he was practically dancing around the school with the boy. He knew when Roger lifted his knees high to run, that he wanted Fleygur to tölt with him. If Roger jogged, Fleygur trotted, and in walk he matched his footsteps exactly, fast or slow.

Roger spent more and more time with Fleygur, and gradually he found the circles on the rope easier to do, especially after Roger had introduced Fleygur to 'carrot-stretches.' Fleygur loved carrot-stretches, bending this way and that to reach the places Roger was holding the carrot, and after he stretched out his muscles they always finished with Fleygur walking backwards, while Roger counted ten steps.

"This is good for your back muscles Fleygur,' Roger said.

Whatever it was for, Fleygur very quickly learnt to count to ten. When Roger said 'ten!" Fleygur stopped for his final carrot.

A couple of times Rowan stopped by while

they were playing, and insisted on planting her lips on the end of his nose, making the strange muffled snorty sound. Once, she brought her brother Kevin with her. He had bright red hair just like hers, only shorter, but he didn't seem interested in making friends with Fleygur, stepping away when he tried to frisk him for treats. Roger looked happy talking to Kevin and Rowan, but he always relaxed more when they left, and he and Fleygur were able to get back to their training.

One evening Fleygur was enjoying a rub down from Roger with the red massage bar when the boy's father pulled into the yard. He got out of the car slowly, his face was stern. Roger hesitated, Fleygur snorted nervously as he picked up the boy's anxiety.

"Roger!" His father was angry. Fleygur knew angry faces, tight and frowning.

"Yes?" Roger said quietly.

"You weren't in school yesterday, and you LIED to me about that fight! Joan saw you leading that horse home last month. You said you hadn't ridden him. You LIED to me!" His father was really angry. Fleygur side-stepped away. Angry humans were scary.

Roger dropped his gaze. Fleygur sensed strange mixed up emotions from the boy.

"Sorry."

"You've bunked off too many times, and now you're lying about riding when I'd said you couldn't! Sorry won't cut it this time."

Roger looked up at his dad and reached out his hand, sliding his fingers into Fleygur's freshly groomed mane. "What do you mean?" His voice sounded thin.

"If I can't trust you to be in school, then the horse will…"

"No!" whispered Roger. Under his mane the boy's fingers gripped Fleygur's neck tightly.

"The horse will have to go," his dad finished.

Roger started to cry.

"I know you think the horse is special Rog, but there can be other horses, later. Joan says this horse is not safe, he had Mr Jones off more than once. Calm one minute and crazy the next. I need you to be safe…I need you…you are all I've got left!" His voice cracked.

"Please Dad, please, not now…," Roger sobbed, "he's not crazy, I promise. We've been working together, he just needs to be understood. Please Dad, no!"

"Sorry, but my mind is made up. The horse has to go."

Roger drew himself up tall.

"I'm sorry I bunked off school. I was wrong to lie to you, and I was wrong about Fleygur too."

"Good," said Roger's dad, "You agree the

horse is too much for you, so–"

"No!" Roger interrupted, "I meant I was wrong about how I was riding Fleygur. I thought if he didn't do what I said, I had to be stronger and make him do what he was told."

"I see," said Roger's dad.

"I didn't need to be stronger. I needed to listen more. I had to work out what he needed."

"Look, this horse psychology is all very well, but I have to think about what's right for you, not the horse. My mind is made up."

"No, Dad, no!" Fleygur flinched as Roger lurched forward and pounded his fists on his dad's chest. Roger's father wrapped his arms around the boy's shoulders, and his son gripped him around the waist, catching his breath between sobs. Fleygur tugged at his rope and tried to reach Roger. The boy needed a huff.

"I'm sorry, I know it's going to be hard to see him go, but you are spending too much time on this animal, neglecting your homework and your school friends–"

"What friends!" shouted Roger, pulling away from his dad. "You don't know anything! You're never here. You don't listen!" The boy's face flushed red with anger, tears running down his cheeks, "Mum would have understood, she promised me my own horse. If she was here she wouldn't let you do this to me!"

"Roger!" His dad raised his voice, "That's enough! The horse goes and that's final."

"NO! You can't–"

"Roger, enough now," said his dad his voice cracking. He turned away, one hand raised to hold his son at bay. As he walked towards the house his shoulders slumped and his head dropped forward.

Roger stared after him, his eyes wide in disbelief.

## CHAPTER 25
### A Special Relationship

After staring at the house for a few moments Roger turned away and kicked at the dirt. Throwing the red massage bar to the floor he walked towards Fleygur and stood in front of him, just gazing at his feet. Fleygur nuzzled at Roger's pockets, but he didn't get a treat. He didn't even get a scratch. Roger just pushed his nose away with his hand and said nothing. Roger felt strange to Fleygur, silent and closed off. Roger untied the rope from the fence and led Fleygur towards the gate, but suddenly the boy stopped and pulling the halter over Fleygur's ears he threw it hard across the field yelling, "Nooooo!"

Fleygur jerked his head up in alarm. He didn't know what this meant. *What does he want? Is this another game?* Fleygur pushed at the boy's back with his nose, but instead of playfully telling him off Roger just walked away, so Fleygur followed him. The boy zig-zagged a couple of times, and Fleygur stayed right on his heels.

"Go away," said Roger, half turning towards Fleygur. "There's no point. Go away." Roger waved his arms at Fleygur's head. Fleygur stopped, but as soon as Roger moved again Fleygur was right there. Something didn't feel right and Fleygur felt nervous, but he knew that being with this boy Roger made him feel safer. They had practiced this game a lot and Fleygur was not going to leave the boy's side now, no matter what.

Roger stopped again, and Fleygur with him. Fleygur bobbed his head nervously. Maybe the boy was going to drive him away with his hands again.

Roger suddenly took a quick step forward. With lightening reaction Fleygur matched him. Then he took another step and Fleygur was on it! Then another, then a jump to the side, and Fleygur twisted quickly side stepping with his front feet to keep with the boy. *That's more like it,* thought Fleygur, *now we are playing!*

Roger let out a little laugh and suddenly sprinted away. Fleygur snorted and chased after him in canter, throwing in a little buck and farting as he went. They both skidded to a halt just before the fence and Roger turned and high-stepped back across the school. Fleygur knew this game too, and launched himself into tölt, lifting his front legs high and gliding alongside the boy, his double-sided mane flying wildly. As they reached the gate at the other end of the schooling area, they could both see the boy's father watching from the porch. Roger hesitated, then he turned and threw his arms around Fleygur's neck.

"I can't lose you, I can't!" he sobbed into Fleygur's mane.

Fleygur was motionless as Roger clung to him, uncertain what these was powerful human feelings meant. Tears streamed down Roger's face as his arms slid from Fleygur's neck and he dropped to the floor. Fleygur stood for a moment, with the sobbing boy as his feet, then stretching his neck he blew softly into the Roger's hair, and nuzzled the top of his head with his upper lip. Then he heard foot steps approaching.

"That looked pretty nice," said the boy's father walking towards them. There was a long pause, as Roger's sobbing subsided.

"I trained him," muttered Roger, not looking up. "He's a good horse."

The boy's father stayed silent, looking down at his son. Then he looked directly at Fleygur. His face was sad, and his eyes red. The boy was not the only one that had been crying. Fleygur swivelled his ears forward trying to work out what this man was going to do, and then he reached towards him with his nose. The man rubbed the end of Fleygur's nose. Then he snatched his hand back quickly, like he hadn't meant to do it, but Roger had seen it, and was quickly on his feet.

"Look," Roger said, taking his dad by his hand. "I found this sore spot here, when I was massaging him, and in his mouth there was a bruise from the bit. It hurt him when I rode!" Roger looked as if he was going to cry again, but he drew in a breath and continued, "...and I worked out something else. He's scared to be away from Hercs. I needed to listen to him more, I had to understand why he did what he did, and help him. He's not crazy. We just need to trust each other more, then he won't be scared."

The boy's father looked at Fleygur again, and then back at Roger. "You need to listen more?"

"Yes."

"And you need to trust each other more?"

"Yes."

"And then you won't be so scared?"

"*Fleygur* won't be," Roger said. Fleygur bobbed his head at the sound of his name.

"Go on," said Roger's dad.

"I've been working with him, every day in half term, and every evening since I went back to school."

"And some days when you should have been in School, apparently!" said his dad quietly.

Roger looked down. "You didn't see because you're never...you have to work so much." Roger's breathing was calmer now, and it seemed to Fleygur that the boy wasn't about to give up, not yet. "We started again, from the beginning, with ground work. I've been watching Mum's DVDs about training horses. I can do it. I can fix this. He's a good horse. Please let him stay. Dad, please?"

Roger's father didn't seem to know what to say, so while he was thinking about it Fleygur snuffled his pockets.

"Roger," his dad said sternly, pushing Fleygur's nose away, "Firstly, you must never lie to me again. Secondly...," he paused.

Roger's eyes flashed with panic and he dropped his gaze, his arms hanging limply at his sides. His eyes closed and he held his breath, like he was bracing himself for something horrible.

Fleygur saw a smile begin to form on the the man's face.

"Secondly...," he continued, "I promise to listen to you more when you tell me about how hard you find it at school."

Roger's head snapped up, his eyes wide.

"How about *we* start again, Rog?"

"What?" said Roger, almost whispering.

"We'll find a way to sort out your problems in school, together," his dad said.

Roger nodded, and he glanced at Fleygur. Fleygur flicked his ears to show he was paying attention, and ready for anything.

"Okay. Let's do a deal. You absolutely promise

me that you will go to school *every* day, and try to make friends, and the horse can stay. How does that sound? Deal?"

"Deal!" said Roger and he threw his arms around his dad.

## CHAPTER 26
### The Best Birthday Present

Every day after that Roger arrived extra early to train with Fleygur before school. Flegyur loved learning new tricks, because Roger used carrots as the reward. It took a lot of carrots before Fleygur learnt how to bow, going down on one knee and stretching his nose to the ground. Fleygur couldn't see the purpose of this manoeuvre, but Roger liked it, and he got carrots, so he wasn't complaining.

Every evening Roger freewheeled his bike back into the yard, ran into the house to change his clothes, and straight back out to Fleygur where he stayed until his dad got home and called him in for tea.

By the time the summer holidays started Fleygur's mouth was fully healed, Roger got back in the saddle and they rambled together over the hills around their home. Fleygur didn't feel the need to run home anymore, he was happy to be with Roger, and now the pain in his back was gone, he barely thought of Jones at all. He had Hercules for company and mutual grooming, and although he was a bit grumpy when Fleygur tried to play-fight, even 'Shorty' could be provoked into a small amount of bucking if Fleygur nipped his legs hard enough. The summer was turning out to be warm and dry and Roger's aura radiated happy feelings. Life was feeling pretty good.

"He's looking better and better," said Roger's dad after watching them train one day.

"He's ace!" Roger said. "I want to enter him in a show. Fleygur's tölt's really good. Philippa, the woman who bred him told me, when she came to Mr Jones's. I can do better than him, I know I can. Fleygur listens to me."

Roger was scratching Fleygur's neck, on the underside, just where he liked it best. He stretched his neck out long and puckered his lips in appreciation.

"One step at a time" his dad said. "So, what do you want to do for your birthday next month?" He asked.

"Nothing," said Roger, looking at his feet.

"Really? I thought you might like to invite a couple of your classmates to go paintballing or something?" said his dad.

"That's expensive, isn't it?" Roger asked.

"Yes, but I could manage it…for a few of you. You've been getting on better in school and making friends, haven't you?

"I dunno who to invite," Roger mumbled.

Fleygur thought things must not being going Roger's way, because he was all excited about how brilliant Fleygur was, and now he was quiet and closed.

"What about that girl Rowan I see hanging about, and her brother, what's his name?"

"Kevin," said Roger.

Roger's eyes brightened suddenly. *The boy's thinking-face,* thought Fleygur.

"Can we camp in the field instead?" Roger said, "...and have a fire, and barbecue? I could show the tricks I taught Fleygur!"

"Great idea!" his dad said.

"I'll invite Charlie, he knows about survival stuff and camping" said Roger.

"Good...and what about that girl, with the fancy mountain bike...what's her name?"

"Jess," Roger said, his bright eyes clouding over.

"Yes, Jess, I'll mention it to her mum."

Roger looked at his dad and then back at his feet. After a moment his dad sighed. "Well, think about it. We can make the rest of the plans later."

Roger watched his father go back to the house. "Jess! She's the last person I want round here," he sighed, resting his hand on Fleygur's mane.

Roger was looking off into the distance, and Fleygur thought he was being ignored, so he gave him a shove with his nose.

"Come on, Fleygur," said Roger, snapping out of his daze, "Let's get you back to Hercules."

The following weekend, as Roger was getting Fleygur ready for their ride, his voice was full of excitement.

"Dad's getting us a trailer for my birthday present. He's collecting it today, I'm getting it early, so I can take you to a Training Clinic! It's the best birthday present ever!"

Hercules snorted, *More hard work, going round in circles, while the trainer explains everything you're doing wrong.*

Fleygur was going to tell Shorty he was just being grumpy again, but Roger's rapid fire excitement interrupted, "… and Dad says, if I do a really good job with you, we can enter the British Championships in September! You and me, Fleygur, we can do it, I know we can."

*Looks like you are going to be a sport horse after all,* Hercules said.

Fleygur, wasn't at all sure that was a good thing anymore. He'd tried that before with Jones, and it didn't go so well.

*I'm a good riding horse, and I do tricks, isn't that enough?* he asked.

*But the boy wants more, he wants to be a champion rider, like his mum,* said Hercules.

Fleygur looked at Roger, his face full of happy

183

wrinkles, as he got ready for their ride.

*He's making quite a good job of horse-talk now,* thought Fleygur, *maybe we can do this horse sport thing, together.*

Later that day, after they got back from their ride, Roger's father returned home towing a dark red and white trailer. Fleygur and Hercules watched as Roger opened and closed all the doors, walked around it, and inspected the inside.

"Perfect," he announced finally to his smiling father. Roger left the ramp at the rear open and grabbed Fleygur's halter. "Come on, we're going to practice loading you. There's only a few days before the clinic."

The last time Fleygur was inside one of these stables-on-wheels was when Jones took him in the boat to the competition. As he looked into the dark space of the trailer, memories crowded his mind; the clanging of the chains, the floor beneath him lurching around, and Jones beating him onto the trailer to come home.

Roger jiggled the lead rope. "Come on, boy, it's okay," he said soothingly. Fleygur took a few steps, but at the bottom of the ramp he stopped, shaking his head to try and release the pressure on the rope.

"What's up with him?" asked Roger's father.

"He's scared," Roger said, "I don't know exactly what happened, but Jones said it was 'a bit rough' on the boat to Germany. I think it was more than that, but Jones wouldn't say. He just made out Fleygur was useless, and it was all his fault that they didn't do well. I don't believe him. I think he did something bad. I could see it in Fleygur's eyes when Jones came near him, after he injured his foot."

Fleygur relaxed as he listened to the sound of Roger's voice, and rested his weight onto one back foot.

"You might well be right. He's got a temper on him, that man," said Roger's dad. "This horse has certainly been okay with you, and Jones has been through a lot of horses. That nice big cob he got for showing, the little ginger thoroughbred mare when he was into Polo, the retired race horse, and there were quite a few before that. Anna didn't like going there to treat his horses, she said they were all scared of him. Your mum could read horses as well as she could people. Maybe that's where you got it from, eh? Your way with horses."

Roger smiled sheepishly as his dad ruffled his hair. "Asif says I talk more to animals than I do to people."

"Who's Asif?"

"He's new, started school last week. He's nice. Helps me with stuff. Can I ask him to my party too?"

"Of course," said his dad, grinning.

Roger turned back to Fleygur. "You going into that trailer, or not?"

*Not,* thought Fleygur, leaning his weight onto his back legs when Roger pulled on the rope again. He wanted to do what Roger asked, but his instincts told him that going into a dark box was a bad idea. Roger sighed. Fleygur sighed too, and leant back further. It looked like they were going to be here for a while so he rested his back foot again.

"So, how are you going to sort this problem?" the boy's father asked, gesturing at Fleygur.

"Slowly," said Roger, giving Fleygur a rub on the nose. "We're not going anywhere today, are we?"

## CHAPTER 27
### Training Clinic

By the time the day of the clinic arrived Fleygur had been in and out of that stable-on-wheels so many times that he didn't even hesitate when Roger asked him to walk on. In fact, Roger just stood at the side of the trailer and threw the rope over Fleygur's back and he walked on of his own accord. Fleygur thought he'd probably go anywhere for Roger - kind, patient, horse-talking Roger. And of course, lots of treats had helped him get over his fear of the trailer too.

Roger's father was a good driver, and the trip was smooth, but when finally the trailer halted, rain was hammering down on the roof, muffling the other sounds and smells from outside. Fleygur couldn't make out where he was and he nodded his head anxiously, his ears flicking forward and back trying to pick up a familiar sound. Then, the little door for humans opened and Roger popped his head in, his hair dripping wet.

"How you doing? Won't be long, just setting up your paddock."

Then he disappeared again. Fleygur twisted

his head around to try and see out, but the sheets of rain formed a shimmering cover over the back of the trailer and he couldn't see. He felt closed in. He didn't like waiting. The smell of the sea air swirled through his memory, and he snorted, *let me out!* He stamped the floor impatiently.

"Okay boy, nearly ready," Roger called from outside the trailer. Roger's voice calmed him a little and a moment later the horse-sized door opened, and light poured in along with the rain. Fleygur trotted down the ramp, loosened his tired muscles with a whole body shake, and looked around. There was a huge part-stone, part-timber barn in front of him, with a couple of horses waiting just inside, standing quietly next to their riders. Someone had thrown rugs over the tops of their saddles to protect them from the rain, making the horses look strangely lumpy. There was a horse further inside the barn being ridden in circles, and Fleygur caught the sound of a familiar voice coming from inside. Relieved to sense something he knew he whinnied, *Hello, I'm here!* The two waiting horses nickered back, their riders turning to check out the noisy new arrival.

"Come on boy," Roger said, taking up the slack in his rope, "into your paddock."

The rain stopped just as Fleygur was getting up from his roll, plastered in mud. As the sun finally broke through the clouds a lorry rumbled along the lane, turned into the yard and pulled up near to Fleygur's paddock. A young man with dark hair jumped down from the cab and quickly set up a paddock next to Fleygur. Then he opened the lorry. The ramp clattered as it hit the floor. Fleygur could hear movement inside. The young man stepped back from the ramp making a gentle clucking noise. Fleygur was stiff and alert, as a magnificent stallion burst from the lorry, prancing down the ramp, strutting around his paddock, and tossing his head, snorting. His dark-slate body rippled, and his shining silver mane tumbled from his neck down onto his shoulders. Fleygur had never seen a silver dapple horse before, or a mane that long! He was sure he must be looking at one of the horses of the Gods. The God horse didn't look happy. He strutted about stamping his feet, and then caught sight of Fleygur. Fleygur nickered a quiet greeting.

"Be nice, Ódinn," said the man, as Ódinn marched up to the edge of his fence to inspect Fleygur at close range, snuffling at his nose. Fleygur felt slightly intimated, and was careful to keep his head lower than Ódinn's so as not to challenge him. Ódinn was strong and confident and Fleygur knew you didn't argue with horses like that.

*You are not a proper Icelandic horse,* snorted Ódinn. *I carried my rider through a blizzard in*

189

*Iceland, with my ears caked in ice, and the trails obliterated by the snow. I've seen mountains explode with fire, and rain ash on our backs.* Ódinn let out a squeal of defiance. *You're no better than a regular fat pony,* and stamping his front foot, Ódinn tossed his head and trotted away.

"Wow!" said Roger, arriving back with a bucket of water, and staring at Ódinn. "Look at him!"

Fleygur shoved Roger's elbow. Water slopped over the edge of the bucket and down Roger's wellies.

"Oi!" Roger said. "Don't worry, I'm not about to swap you!" He gave Fleygur an affectionate scratch. "Let's get you tacked up for our lesson. We're next."

"Is this Fleygur, then?" asked the tall young man, as he slipped a halter onto Ódinn, "Jones's horse?"

"He's not Jones's horse any more. He's mine." Roger replied with a smile.

"You'll not get far in competition with that horse," said the young man. Looking Fleygur up and down. "He's the wrong type. Too stocky, and, well…fat. And his legs are too short. I'm sure he's just right for you though." He smiled at Roger, but it didn't look that friendly to Fleygur.

Roger turned away from the man. He swallowed hard and blinked some tears from his

190

eyes. Then he set about brushing Fleygur with firm determined strokes.

The young man stood there for a while, looking at Roger's back, then shrugged his shoulders, and led Ódinn over to their own trailer.

Fleygur looked around at the other sporty, fit looking horses in nearby paddocks, with their long legs and wiry bodies. *They must be starving, he thought, don't they know how important it is to keep an extra layer of fat, in case the food runs out!*

"Making friends?" asked Roger's father, as he walked up to them.

"Mmmm," said Roger, not turning around.

"Come on, on you get. Philippa's waiting for you."

As they entered the indoor school Fleygur recognised the shape and movement of Philippa, standing in the middle and nickered a greeting. Philippa turned around smiling.

"Well hello, Fleygur! Aren't you looking… um…well!" she said, eyeing up his belly. And nice to meet you again Roger," she said, "I've been hearing all about the great things you've been doing with my Fleygur here. Shall we get started?"

Fleygur tried hard to tölt all the way round, but the arena was small and tölting in a small circle was much harder than in straight lines. After just few circles he started to feel tired, and stopped.

"Use your lower legs, Roger," Philippa called from the centre of the arena.

*Hercules was right,* thought Fleygur, *this is hard. We're not even going anywhere!*

Roger tried to push Fleygur on with his legs, but Fleygur thought the boy must be getting tired too, because he didn't seem like he really meant it, so Fleygur didn't move.

"Maybe there's something wrong with him," Roger said to Philippa. "He's not like this at home."

"It's harder for him here. It's not like when you are hacking out. You have to keep asking for tölt. Let's check him out," Philippa said, walking over to Fleygur. She checked the fit of his bridle and saddle, and felt down his legs. "He is a bit overweight," she said looking up at Roger, "It won't help him."

"I rescued him. He was all alone in a huge field of long grass. It's not my fault," Roger said.

"I didn't say it was your fault," said Philippa gently. "I know all about what happened at the competition in Germany, from friends who were there. And your dad's just told me about what happened after. I'm very glad you found him Roger."

Philippa leaned over towards Fleygur's head and cupped her hands around her mouth, and whispered into Fleygur's ear.

"You need to help your boy out here. I don't think you know how lucky you are to have him." Then she stepped away.

"He's fine," she said to Roger. "His tack and his legs all check out. Just ask him to walk on again, but you must make sure you really mean it. If you're not sure, he won't be either."

"What did you say to him? Roger asked.

"Ah," said Philippa, "that's between me and him."

Fleygur wasn't too sure exactly what Philippa had meant about helping, but he had appreciated the break, and this time when Roger squeezed his legs onto Fleygur's sides Fleygur felt a new burst of energy through the boy's body, and he stepped out smartly. Very soon Roger was smiling again.

"See I told you!" said Philippa, at the end of the lesson. "I think you make a really good partnership."

Fleygur lowered his head, breathing hard. The sun was hot and he was tired, but Roger was scratching one of his favourite spots, just in front of his saddle, and Fleygur could feel Roger's happiness. Philippa had a wrinkled up face, so he was sure he had done well. He definitely felt like he'd worked hard enough, and looked forward to his roll and some hay!

"You're doing a really good job." Philippa continued. "You should be proud. You just need to get his weight down and work on his fitness. I'll look forward to seeing you at the British Championships!"

## CHAPTER 28
### Roger's Birthday

The sky was a clear bright blue with just faint wisps of cloud smeared across its face. It was late August, and although Fleygur could sense the coming autumn on the breeze, the day was already getting warm. Roger appeared in the porch and wedged a bacon sandwich in his mouth while he pulled on his wellies. He grabbed Fleygur's halter from its hook and headed across the yard to the gate, where Fleygur was waiting. Maybe he would get a treat. Sometimes he did and sometimes he didn't, but it was always worth hanging out here just in case. Today turned out to be a 'didn't' day. Roger just rubbed Fleygur's face instead. Fleygur didn't mind. He liked scratches too.

"It's my birthday today Fleygur," Roger said, but he didn't seem too happy about it. He absentmindedly twisted his fingers into Fleygur's mane, gazing up to the hill with a faraway look in his eyes, like he was looking for a missing herd-mate. Fleygur looked to the hill too, but there was no-one there.

"Don't take too long with his training," the

boy's father called from the open kitchen window. "We have to get those tents up."

"Okay," Roger called back. "Why did he have to go and invite Jess to MY birthday weekend?" he grumbled.

Fleygur pulled away as Roger was twisting his mane a little more than was comfortable. Roger huffed, so Fleygur sighed too. Roger may not be paying attention to him, but he was totally tuned into his boy. Roger laughed.

"You always do that, you funny pony. Come on, let's get some practice, you've got a special job later. I want you to be ready. We're going to show that girl a thing or two about fluffy ponies, aren't we?"

Fleygur wasn't sure which fluffy ponies Roger meant, but he happily ambled after him to the schooling area. After their training session, and having got good and scruffy rolling in the dust, Fleygur wandered over to where Hercules was watching Roger and his father struggling with some sticks and flapping sheets. The wind had picked up, and the sheets didn't seem to be doing what they were supposed to, but by lunchtime four pointy-topped tents were arranged around some benches and a small pile of wood. Roger grabbed a brush and headed back to Fleygur. He seemed to have cheered up a bit, and after a quick body brush he set about pulling the twigs from Fleygur's mane.

"We need to have you polished up for your audience," he said. The boy's voice sounded nervous-excited. *Like when I go somewhere I don't know for the first time*, Fleygur thought.

Fleygur had the feeling something important was about to happen.

Late in the afternoon the guests arrived. Rowan was first, bright eyed and excited, her red wavy hair bouncing as she ran across the yard to the horses. She climbed up on the bottom rail and reached out to rub Hercules on the nose. Her brother Kevin, much quieter than his sister, made straight for the camp, and started poking at the fire pit.

"Fleygur is so cute!" Rowan beamed at Roger, who went slightly pink in the cheeks and looked down at the floor.

Rowan reminded Fleygur of his over enthusiastic little brother, Ragnar, when he was a gangly foal, leaping about the place, and still learning his horse-manners from their mum. Fleygur pawed at the ground to attract the girl's attention. Maybe she had some treats in her pocket. He didn't want to miss out. But Rowan was excitedly firing questions at Roger about how horses are able to stand up in moving trailers, and why they didn't fall over when you go round

197

roundabouts.

Fleygur heard Roger's slight intake of breath and flicked an ear in his direction. He was watching Jess, getting out of her mum's car with a snarly grin already plastered on her face. Anytime Roger moved or spoke Fleygur checked him out, just in case he was about to be fed, or if there was a signal that they were moving. It was always a good idea to keep a careful eye on your herd-mates, and Roger was part of his herd. Roger's breathing shortened slightly as Jess approached.

"Well, ain't that cute," she drawled, looking at Rowan. "Your own Barbie doll for your fluffy-wuffy ponies."

Roger's face reddened.

"Shut up, Jess!" Rowan said, stepping down from the fence. "It's Roger's birthday, try being nice for once!" She beamed at Roger, who went even more red.

Finally, Asif and Charlie arrived in quick succession. Asif's parents stopping for a quick word with Roger's father over the yard gate, and Charlie on his own and on foot, carrying a huge backpack.

"Cool," said Asif, having a quick scout around the tents, picking out one and slinging his sleeping bag inside. "This one's mine."

Fleygur was standing at the gate with Hercules, watching the rest of children scrabbling about, running in and out of tents and arguing about who was sleeping where. Fleygur thought they looked like a gang of foals, play-fighting and nose-biting to see who was boss.

"Come on then you lot," said Roger's father "We've got more wood to gather for the camp fire. No fire, no food!"

As the children trooped after the boy's father towards the wooded area at the top of the field, Roger lagged behind, giving Fleygur a scratch behind his ears.

"I guess it won't be so bad," he said grudgingly.

Fleygur watched, as Roger jogged up the hill to catch up with the others, then wandered off with Hercules to graze. The noise of the children's shouting slowly faded into the distance.

Finally, the small gang arrived back with arms full of sticks, and Charlie and Roger dragging long branches behind them. Roger's father chopped up the branches and supervised the building and lighting of the camp fire. The fire started spitting as the damp wood caught alight, and flecks of burning bark wafted up into the air. Fleygur snorted, walking to the other side of the field, with Hercules trailing after him. Smoke and fire were dangerous, and to be avoided at all costs. The humans didn't seem bothered by it though, and once the smoke subsided the children sat wrapping potatoes in silver foil, and the boy's father placed them carefully in the hot embers at the base of the fire.

"Okay," he said, "those baked potatoes will take an hour and half at least, so plenty of time for your demo Rog!"

As Roger walked over to Fleygur with his halter, Fleygur could feel that the boy had his 'work head' on. He slipped his halter on and led him to the centre of the schooling area. Roger removed Fleygur's halter and took several steps backwards. Fleygur followed the boy's movements with his eyes and ears, watching for the slightest signal.

The children clambered up onto the bottom rung of the fence, and Roger's father leant on the gate, with a soft smile on his face.

Everyone was waiting for something to happen, including Fleygur.

## CHAPTER 29
### Putting on a Show

"Right, I'm going to show you some moves I've taught Fleygur," Roger said.

"You'll have to speak up," his dad called. "We can't hear you."

Roger cleared his throat. "We're going to show you some moves," he said. He turned to face Fleygur and let out a long slow breath.

Fleygur focussed all his attention on the boy, waiting for him move. Roger lifted his right foot, and placed it deliberately in front of him. Fleygur lifted his left front foot and stepped back. Roger lifted his left foot, but before he replaced it on the ground, Fleygur had already stepped back with his right. Slowly, moving together, Fleygur stepped in time with his boy across the schooling area. A slight change in the way Roger's body leant, and Fleygur was ready for a switch of direction. Roger suddenly started running backwards, and Fleygur chased after him, his mane flying around as he jogged after the boy. Fleygur loved this game, and tossed his head with excitement, his long thick mane flying around.

"Woo hoo!" called Rowan, clapping her hands.

"It's not so impressive," said Jess, "My dog can do that!"

Roger didn't respond to Jess's taunt, all his focus was on Fleygur, just as he was tuned to the boy's every move as they zig-zagged back across the school, Fleygur side-stepping alongside Roger.

*Side-stepping is easy for humans*, thought Fleygur, as Roger went faster and faster. *They only have two legs!* But Fleygur didn't miss a step, and as they reached the end of the school, Roger's face broke into a grin. Suddenly he darted way from Fleygur laughing. Fleygur let out a squeal of excitement as he raced after Roger, his muscles rippling as he added a few twisty bucks along the way. The watching children jumped back from the fence as Roger reached it, quickly followed by Fleygur sliding to a halt in a cloud of dust. Fleygur snorted at the dust and turned to see what Roger was going to do next.

Roger picked up Fleygur's bridle from the fence and slipped it on, leaving the reins looped over Fleygur's neck. They turned together and walked quietly away side by side, Roger resting an arm on Fleygur's neck. Fleygur was glad for the chance to get his breath back. Then Roger grabbed a handful of mane and swung up onto Fleygur's back. With no saddle Fleygur could feel every tiny movement in the boy's body, as they first walked, and then tölted around the schooling area, first slow, then faster.

"Bet your dog can't do this!" Roger called to Jess, who despite herself was watching slightly opened mouthed as they flew past. When she saw the others looking at her she quickly closed her mouth and gave a little shrug.

"That was tölt!" announced Roger, sounding full of confidence, "Me and Fleygur are going to win the Icelandic Horse British Championships with that tölt."

Roger circled Fleygur into the centre of the school and lightly tapped his shoulder with his hand. Fleygur knew what this meant. Carefully he tucked his right foreleg back, and leant backwards on his hind legs, dipping into a deep bow, his nose almost touching the ground. Roger swung a leg over his head and jumped to the ground, one arm across his body, joining Fleygur with his own bow.

As all the children burst into applause, and Roger's father beamed at his son, Roger reached into his pocket and slipped Fleygur a crunchy treat. This was Fleygur's favourite part, that and the happy feelings flowing from his boy next to him.

"Who wants to sit on him?" asked Roger. "I can get his saddle."

"Me, Me, Me!" Rowan's hand shot up in the air. She was so bubbling over in excitement, that Fleygur couldn't help but fidget himself as Roger helped her get on.

"Easy, boy," Roger spoke softly to him, walking by his side as they took a few careful turns around the school. Rowan was not very balanced, and Fleygur was careful to move slowly so as not to drop her. Eventually the girl settled down, but Fleygur was relieved when the little bundle of energy finally got off.

As Rowan ran over to where Kevin and Asif were poking at the fire with sticks, Roger led Fleygur to where Jess was still watching from the fence.

"Do you want a go?" he asked.

Fleygur sensed instant panic in the girl, and she suddenly went very pale. He snorted nervously.

"I...I...I don't like horses," Jess said quickly, glancing over at the others.

Roger watched her for a moment. He looked towards the others by the fire, and then back at Jess, like he was seeing something for the first time.

"You'll be fine, I'll hold him," he said gently, in the voice he usually used for helping Fleygur to relax. Feeling that his performance must be nearly over, Fleygur dropped his head and let out a big sigh.

Roger chuckled. "See, he's practically asleep." He paused. "I won't tell the others you're scared," he whispered.

Jess's eyes widened as she stared back at Roger. Fleygur thought she looked like she was thinking of bolting for a moment. Then, her eyes softened, and very quietly she said, "Okay."

As Roger helped Jess's foot into the stirrup Fleygur could feel the girl shaking, but Roger's presence and calm voice was almost hypnotic. Fleygur couldn't understand what frightened the girl so much, but she must have been soothed by Roger's voice too, because finally the shaking subsided and she was sitting motionless on his back. As they meandered around Jess stopped holding her breath and gripping with her legs. As she relaxed, Fleygur, relaxed too and took bigger slower strides. This was starting to feel good, and Fleygur thought the girl might even have a wrinkly-happy face. Roger turned and smiled up at Jess.

"You're doing good," he said.

"You can help me give them hay, if you want." Roger said to Jess, after she had dismounted.

Fleygur pricked his ears as he watched them walk towards the hay-barn.

"It means they will stay near the camp tonight," Roger added. "It's fun camping out with the horses. I like hearing them munching in the night."

This was fine with Fleygur, he liked munching in the night, and extra rations were welcome at any time.

*Now you know what I had to put up with when I was younger,* said Hercules as they tucked into their hay. *Endless children hopping on and off, using my reins to hold themselves up, and bouncing along with no thought to my poor back.*

*Children aren't so bad,* thought Fleygur, as he gazed at the little figures, their faces lit up by the dancing fire.

*You've never met Jones,* Fleygur told Hercules.

*Roger is the sort of human a horse can be mates with,* thought Fleygur, *and I'm going to make him a champion rider one day too, just as the boy wants.*

## CHAPTER 30
### Ride like a Viking!

The following Sunday, as Fleygur was grazing next to Hercules, a blue van pulled up in the gateway. A window in one of the doors opened, and a man peered out, scanning around their yard. Fleygur lifted his head from grazing to watch them. *Maybe they were coming in. Maybe they had treats?*

Just then the front door of the house opened and Roger's voice drifted across the yard as he called back into the house. "Okay, I'll be back by three, bye!"

Fleygur and Hercules turned to the house and nickered together, *"Roger! Treats?"*

As Roger came out of the house, carrying saddlebags, the van pulled away smartly. The boy glanced towards the engine sound, but the van had already disappeared behind the hedge.

Since Roger's birthday the previous week they had been out every day, roaming around the lanes and tracks. Roger's father seemed more relaxed about them going out, and had stopped asking Roger to promise they wouldn't ride on the roads. As long as Roger had his hat and his phone with him, his father was happy.

Fleygur could smell the sandwiches in the saddle bags, and if he wasn't mistaken, and he usually wasn't, there were some of his favourite treats too.

"Come on, Fleygur, we are going up the big hill today," Roger announced.

Fleygur's sleek summer coat was shining in the summer sun. August had been hot and dry, and today was no different, but Fleygur could feel pressure building in the air as Roger tacked him up, and feeling a little worried he pawed at the dusty ground.

"You're keen" Roger said, affectionally rubbing Fleygur's ears. Roger grabbed a handful of Fleygur's mane and jumped up into the saddle. "Let's go!" he said.

Picking up on the hum of Roger's energy Fleygur set off at a brisk walk, *See you later, Shorty,* he whinnied to Hercules, who was now so used to them coming and going that he didn't even bother to look up from his grazing, and simply flicked his ears in Fleygur's direction.

Fleygur quick marched up the track and into the trees, then following a narrow bridleway over the hill behind the house they made their way down into the next valley. As they rode alongside the stream Fleygur swished his tail crossly at a horse-fly that was trying to land on his back.

"Ow!" yelled Roger suddenly, slapping a horse-fly from his arm. "Let's get out of here," he said, leaning forward and urging Fleygur into a canter. The horse-flies loved the shady path by the stream and Fleygur was glad to get away from the nasty biting things. With the breeze blowing through his mane he galloped up the the side of the valley and out of the tree cover towards the hilltop. After his initial burst of speed, and as the hill got steeper, Fleygur began puffing hard. Just when he thought he needed to stop, Roger sat back in the saddle, "Easy boy," he murmured, and Fleygur gratefully slowed to walk, dropping his head low. It was good to have a rider who knew when he'd had enough.

After a few steps he felt the halt signal through Roger's body and as they stopped the boy swung his leg over Fleygur's head and jumped off. Roger led him over the last stretch of ground to the very top of hill and they paused for a moment, looking out at the rolling hills stretching ahead of them, the patchwork fields of browns, yellows and greens filling the lowlands as far as they could see.

*This is a good place,* Fleygur thought, *lots of things to eat, and no chance of anything dangerous sneaking up on us.*

"Time for a rest," Roger said, unbuckling Fleygur's girth and sliding his saddle off. He propped the saddle up on its end, and unclipped the reins from Fleygur's bridle.

"You won't go far, will you boy?" It was more of an instruction than a question, but Fleygur had no intention of going anywhere. He dropped his head to crop the grass, keeping his ears on Roger, to make sure he didn't go anywhere unexpectedly either.

As Fleygur grazed, Roger lay on the ground nearby. He tucked his hands under his head, elbows pointing out, and closed his eyes.

A light breeze began and the air cooled. Fleygur was feeling well and truly rested when Roger finally rolled onto his front, propping his head up with his hands. "Oh, look at that," he said, "pretty sure that's one of those flowers that Dad goes on about."

Fleygur wondered what Roger was looking at and stepped a little closer, still grazing.

Roger reached out his hand and gently touched the purple petals.

"They're supposed to be quite rare," he said, reaching into his pocket to retrieve his phone.

As the boy raised his phone to snap a photo, Fleygur reached over and snatched the flower into his mouth. It tasted bitter.

"Fleygur!" Roger gasped, "You're not supposed to…," but he was already laughing, and Fleygur couldn't quite see what the problem was. Roger had pointed out a tasty treat, and Fleygur had eaten it.

Roger scrambled to his feet and turned to Fleygur, but the boy's eyes were drawn to the horizon.

"Uh-oh," he said.

Fleygur followed his gaze. Big black clouds were tumbling over the mountains in the distance, and the stiffening breeze was sweeping them swiftly in their direction. A distant rumble of thunder seemed to jolt Roger into action.

"We can't be out in a thunderstorm," he said, grabbing the saddle and throwing it over Fleygur's back, quickly buckling up the girth. He clipped on the reins and leapt into the saddle. "Come on Fleygur, we have to ride for home!"

Fleygur walked down the steep hill as fast as he dared, and quickly covered the uneven ground in the bottom of the valley as they fast-tölted past the stream until they reached the last hill before home. The storm was catching up with them, and the rain fell in big slow dollops. Roger hesitated at the fork in the path. The lower path was the way they'd come, and Fleygur knew this was the short way home. But it was narrow, and they would have to walk. The path over the hill was exposed but wide, and they could go really fast. Roger pointed Fleygur to the higher path. Picking up on Roger's excitement Fleygur flew up the hill like he was being hunted by the wind that whipped up behind them. As they reached the top the cloud descended around them and they were riding through a thick damp soup of swirling grey mist. The raindrops came faster and harder. A deep rumble of thunder, closer than the last, caused Fleygur to quicken his pace. He couldn't see more than a few feet in front of him but he galloped on, trusting his Viking horse instinct to find the safe places to put his feet.

As they raced through the elements Fleygur squinted his eyes against the stinging raindrops. Fleygur wasn't frightened of this storm though. The boy was urging him on, full of confidence. Roger was dreaming about being a Viking, riding into battle, and Fleygur knew it. He could feel it. *A Viking horse, that's me,* he thought, and he galloped for all he was worth.

At the end of the track they slowed for the descent towards home. They were both soaked, but Roger was smiling. He bent forward over Fleygur's neck and wrapped his arms around him,

"That was amazing Fleygur," he whispered. "You are ready for the Championships, my Little Viking Horse."

Fleygur pricked his ears. *Little Viking Horse! The name my mother gave me. How did Roger know? He is the one, he must be the one,* Fleygur thought. *My mate Roger.*

## CHAPTER 31
### Thieves in the Night!

A couple of weeks later, when the summer days were starting to shorten, Fleygur was feeling fitter than ever. He and Roger were training for the British Championships nearly every day, and Fleygur knew the pattern of the class they were going to ride as well as the paths around his home. Slow tölt, trot, walk, canter, and then fast tölt, flying like the wind. Roger always 'whooped' when they did this bit.

"One final lesson with Philippa tomorrow," said Roger, as he turned Fleygur out into the field one night, "and the week after, the British Championships!" Roger hugged Fleygur hard and Fleygur could feel the boy's heart pounding with excitement.

Fleygur munched happily on the long grass as the sun went down, with the comforting sound of Hercules grazing nearby. Fleygur was content with his life, and with his boy, and now they were going to be champions too.

As darkness fell Roger's father was hitching the trailer to his big black car.

"Right, the tent can go on the roof rack in the morning. Have you definitely packed everything you need, Rog?"

"Yup. Saddle, bridle, brushes, hoof pick…" Roger recited, counting on his fingers, "…my hat - over by his halter…boots, hay, carrots—"

Fleygur nickered. He knew the word carrots very well.

Roger laughed. "You get packed tomorrow, Fleygur! He's really fit, and not so round. I hope Philippa will be happy with him."

"I'm sure she'll be very pleased," said his father, "Now, it's after nine, time for your bed! We've an early start tomorrow."

Long after the lights in the house were switched off, and Fleygur and Hercules had moved to the far end of the paddock to graze under the trees, Fleygur heard the distant sound of an engine. There were no headlights, but he could definitely hear something approaching down the lane. Then it stopped in the gateway to their yard. Fleygur lifted his head towards the sound. *What's that?*

*Nothing*, snorted Hercules. *It's always nothing in the middle of the night. Either it's nothing, or nothing you should involve yourself in.*

Fleygur was about to start eating again when he heard the sound of a foot step crunch on

214

gravel, and then another. He snapped his head up. *It's not nothing*, said Fleygur. *It's humans, in our yard!* Fleygur took a step towards the yard.

*Stay away*, snorted Hercules, flattening his ears and waving his nose irritably at Fleygur. *Humans sneaking around in the night are up to no good. I know. I've had enough trouble with young louts trying to climb on my back for a laugh. Keep out of sight.*

Fleygur bobbed his head nervously.

"Here it is," said a low voice.

Fleygur flicked his ears and glanced across at Hercules who was still grazing, stubbornly insisting that nothing was happening.

"Can you start it?" said another voice.

"Expect so. Hey, that's handy, the trailer's attached already. That'll save time!"

Fleygur snorted. He didn't like this.

"What about the ponies, shall we take 'em?" said the first voice.

"Don't be daft! What would you do with a couple of ponies? Now let's get the Land Rover and the trailer and get out of here."

"But—"

"We've got ten minutes to meet Sam at the gates to that posh place and load up the quad bike. Quit wittering about them ponies."

When the engine of the big car started, Fleygur trotted over to the gate. This was a sound he knew, Roger's father arriving or leaving home.

But he stopped abruptly at the enormous crash, as the car smashed straight through the closed gates and then turned sharp left up the lane, the trailer lurching and weaving behind it. Almost at once the upstairs lights in the house came on, and moments later Roger's father appeared in the front doorway, wearing only pyjama bottoms and rubbing his eyes. Roger appeared behind him, and tried to squeeze past.

"Stay there," said his dad. "Let me check it out."

But Roger took no notice and pushing past his father, he ran barefoot across the yard and putting one hand on the top of the gate, he jumped over.

"Damn it," said his father, waving a torch around the yard. "They got the Land Rover and trailer. Straight through the gates. What a mess!"

Fleygur trotted towards Roger nickering a greeting. The strange people, and the noise had spooked him and he was glad to see the boy.

"Mind my feet, Fleygur!" said Roger, putting a hand on Fleygur's chest to stop him coming too close. He grabbed Fleygur's halter from the gate and slipped it over his head. Throwing a rope around Hercules's neck he led them both to the stables. Roger switched on the lights and inspected each of them, running his hands down their legs and over their backs.

"They're both fine," Roger called, guiding Hercules into the stable and bolting the door.

"Okay, I'll call the Police," his father said, turning back to the house.

*I told you it was trouble,* said Hercules, *I know when humans are up to no good. But no harm done.*

Fleygur wasn't at all sure about that. He had a bad feeling, and Roger had one of those looks on his face. The look that meant something was not going his way.

Roger was helping his dad to nail the gates back together when a police car pulled up in the gateway and a woman got out. She made notes in a little black book as she talked to Roger's father,

"Organised gangs stealing to order. They've been scouting the area for a few weeks now," she said.

"I bet they wanted our trailer to put what they stole in!" said Roger.

"Quite likely," the officer replied. "We've had several reports of two guys in a blue van in places they shouldn't be. You'll not be seeing your Landy any time soon I'm afraid. It will probably be out of the country, or broken up for parts by tomorrow. Sorry. I'd better get off, there's sure to be some more break-ins before the night's over."

After the police officer had left, Roger barely said a word, but as he helped with the gates, he kept glancing at his dad. Fleygur thought the boy would burst if he didn't speak soon.

"What about the show?" Roger asked sheepishly, like he knew the answer already.

"That's the least of my worries right now," said his dad, not looking up.

"But Dad, I have to go, I have to...Fleygur is ready and—!"

"Rog, how on earth am I supposed to even get to work?" his dad snapped, "I can't just magic transport up from nowhere you know." His tone softened. "And even if I could pick up a cheap runabout, we can't afford a new trailer too. I'm really sorry, your competition plans will have to wait."

"But I have to!" Roger pleaded. Fleygur thought he might start leaking tears, but the boy drew a deep breath and held himself together. "I told everyone in school we are going to the Championships, I can't wait another whole year! I wanted to win, with Flegyur. I wanted to do it in memory of Mum..." the boy's voice broke off.

"Oh Rog," his dad said sadly, slipping his arm round Roger's shoulder and hugging him. "I'm sorry. She'd be very proud. I know you've worked hard, but we just can't do it. Let's plan it together, for next year."

Roger and his dad stood hugging for a few moments, before his dad eased him away and gently wiped a stray tear from Roger's cheek.

"Now pop the horses back in the field," he said, " while I tie up these gates. I'll call Philippa in the morning and let her know we are not coming."

In silence, his head bowed, Roger untied Fleygur's rope and started towards the field. Fleygur trailed after him. Sadness was oozing from the boy, and Fleygur knew it was not the time to hassle him for treats.

Suddenly, Fleygur caught a faint ashy smell on the cooling night air. He followed the scent trail with his nose, turning his head towards it, and pricked his ears. Roger followed his gaze.

"What's that?" Roger said, pointing to an orange glow over the tree tops.

"A Fire! A big one too," said his father. "Looks like it's Jones' place, and that's a lot of smoke. Could be the hay-barn."

"Bet those thieves have done over Jones's, he's got tons of stuff up there," Roger said. Then he drew in a sharp breath, "The horses!"

Fleygur snorted in response to Roger's alarm. He couldn't sense any danger nearby, but the boy clearly thought something was wrong.

I'll call the fire brigade," said the boy's father, heading back towards the house.

"The horses..." Roger repeated, almost whispering. He looked at his father as he disappeared into the house, and then at Fleygur. Fleygur stiffened in readiness.

Roger was about to do something.

# CHAPTER 32
## The Fire

The ominous glow was getting brighter over the trees, and thick black smoke was bellowing up into the night sky. Fleygur could taste the bitter smoke in the air. Roger quietly tied the loose end of the lead rope to the side of Fleygur's halter, and flipped the rope over his head. Hesitating, he glanced back at the house, then he grabbed Fleygur's mane and leapt onto Fleygur bareback. Roger had only ever done this in the field before, but now he bent forward, threading his fingers into Fleygur's mane and gripped tightly. Fleygur could feel the mix of fear and excitement pumping though Roger's body, and was ready to spring into action as Roger whispered urgently, "Come on now Fleygur, GO!"

Fleygur leapt forward, accelerating at such speed that his metal shoes slid on the concrete yard like a cartoon pony running on the spot. A split second later he got traction and they were off, clattering out through the gate at a gallop, just as Roger's father came running back out of the house.

"ROGER! Get back here…!" But his voice was drowned out by the drumming of Fleygur's hooves on the lane. Fleygur felt Roger sliding back and he slowed a little, but Roger gripped his mane more tightly and pushed him on,

"Come on, Fleygur, gallop like the wind."

Roger's heart was racing, and Fleygur's own heartbeat quickened in response. Something was badly wrong. He stuck his nose forward and lengthened his stride. Flat out gallop was hard on the tarmac lane, and Fleygur slipped more than once, but Roger showed no sign of wanting to slow down.

As they galloped down the long driveway towards to Jones's yard, Fleygur could hear the dogs barking, and Lina and Jinks thundering around their field, calling. Fleygur summoned enough breath to whinny, *I'm coming!* Lina whinnied back, quickly followed by Beanie's screaming call, from inside the barn! Fleygur could sense the panic of the other horses, and tried to turn to join Lena and Jinks, but Roger pushed him on through the gates and into the yard, where they slid to a halt. Fleygur was sweating and puffing. His eyes wide, he spun around trying to make sense of what was happening. Roger slipped from Fleygur's back and looked at the two horses charging about in the field.

"Beanie and Ginger *are* in the barn!" Roger

said, his voice trembling. Fleygur snorted. The acrid smoke was already burning his nostrils, and the crackling flames were getting louder, punctuated by explosions from within the barn. Suddenly Roger darted towards a heap of clothes piled in front of the barn doors.

"Mr Jones, Mr Jones!" he yelled, shaking the heap. Fleygur startled as the pile of clothes moved and Jones pulled himself up to on his hands and knees, coughing.

"I got a hold of one of them," he said, "but he got away. Then his mate threw something right into the barn and they legged it, I chased after..."

"The horses!" Roger interrupted, pulling on Jones's shirt, trying to drag him towards the barn.

"I tried already...the smoke's too thick. It's too late!" Jones said, pulling away from Roger, and breaking into a fit of coughing.

Beanie screamed again from inside the barn, quickly followed by Ginger's panicked high pitched calling. Fleygur could hear kicking and splintering wood. Roger ran towards the barn doors, and covering his mouth with his arm, he disappeared inside.

Fleygur nickered, tossing his head and turning in circles. He wanted to run, but Roger...

"Idiot boy!" growled Jones, as he stumbled into the barn after Roger. Seconds later Beanie and Ginger came clattering out through the doorway, dragging a swirl of thick black smoke behind them. They swerved either side of Fleygur and thundered through the yard gates and up the drive. Fleygur swivelled on his hunches to join them. Flee, his instinct told him, flee!

"FLEYGUR!" Roger's voice from inside the barn made him hesitate. Then, there he was, stumbling out of the barn, his clothes blackened with ash.

"Fleygur!" his voice rasped from the smoke, "I need you."

Roger grabbed Fleygur's rope and turned back towards the burning barn. Fleygur took a step forwards, but when he saw they were heading for the fire he sunk his hind legs down and stopped. *I'm not going in there!*

"Please Fleygur, I can't do it on my own!" Roger pleaded, but gripped with fear Fleygur leant backwards against the rope.

Roger desperately looked around, then he pulled his sweat-shirt off, dunked it in the water trough, and threw it over Fleygur's head, covering his face. Fleygur pulled back in panic. He was blind! But Roger spoke to him.

"Easy, boy, easy."

Fleygur could still sense the fear, but now Roger sounded calm, determined.

"Come on, Fleygur, you have to do this!" he said.

Feeling the tug on the rope, and with Roger leading, Fleygur gingerly stepped forward, little by little. The smoke grew thicker, and the crackling louder. Fleygur sensed they were inside the barn and his muscles trembled as he fought the urge to spin around and run. Only Roger's voice, and his hand stroking his neck, kept Fleygur moving forward. Then, Fleygur felt a rope being secured around his neck and chest.

"Come on, Fleygur, pull!" said Roger.

Fleygur tried to step forward, but something heavy was attached to the other end of the rope. He froze, not knowing what to do.

"Come on, Fleygur, PULL!" shouted Roger, his voice breaking into a cough.

Fleygur's heart pumped hard. He could feel panic rising in Roger. He wanted to flee, but he was blind. The roar and crackle of the fire was terrifying, but he couldn't move. Roger sobbed and sunk to his knees. "I can't breathe," he croaked.

Suddenly the covering on Fleygur's face was gone and he could see the open barn doors in front of them. The doors were ablaze, but between them Fleygur could see moonlight reflecting on the water trough in the yard. Now he could see his escape Fleygur leant into the rope and pulled with all his might. With the boy hanging on to his mane and dragging a dead weight behind him, they approached the doors. Thick black smoke sank lower and lower, until he could no longer see the silvery moon outside.

Fleygur gave one final heave into the blindness of the smoke and they were out!

Roger let go of Fleygur's mane and flopped to the ground just as his dad arrived in the yard, wobbling and oversized on his son's bike. The bike clattered to the floor as he dropped it and ran towards them, his face red and angry. Fleygur stepped back as he reached them, but ignoring Fleygur he swept Roger into his arms and burst into tears.

"You stupid boy, you could have been killed!"

"I'm sorry, I'm sorry, but we had to save the horses…and Jones, he collapsed, I couldn't move him!" Roger sobbed.

Roger's dad quickly turned Jones who was lying behind Fleygur, with the rope still knotted around his ankles. He put his cheek against Jones's face, and took his wrist between his finger and thumb.

"Is he dead?" asked Roger, his voice small and faint.

"No," said his dad, rolling Jones carefully onto his side. "He's still breathing."

Fleygur lowered his head to sniff the figure on the ground. Jones didn't seem so scary now, crumpled on the floor, covered in ash. Jones groaned, and then coughed, blinking open his eyes he looked up at Fleygur.

"You!" He rasped, and broke into a fit of coughing.

Roger and his dad held each other in a tight hug as the fire raged behind them. Fleygur twitched at the crackles and bangs from the barn, and Roger reached out to rub Fleygur's forehead. Fleygur nuzzled at the boy's arm with his lips.

The sound of distant sirens grew louder as two fire engines sped towards them, blue lights flashing. Ahead of them came Beanie and Ginger, thundering back up the drive, their eyes wild with fear.

"We'd better get those horses in that field. Quick, this way…"

Roger's father ran to open a nearby gate, and Roger grabbed Fleygur's rope and quickly led him across the path of the panicking horses. As Fleygur and Roger ran into the field, Beanie and Ginger swung around to join them, and Roger's father closed the gate behind them.

Fleygur dropped for a roll and Roger laughed when he got up and shook the dust off,

"You're even dirtier than before, with all that ash."

Fleygur didn't care, his itching was eased.

"Fleygur saved us all," Roger said, as they

watched the firefighters with their hoses trained on the barn. "The horses and Mr Jones. He galloped all the way. He came into the barn for me and pulled Jones out. I couldn't have done it on my own. Jones would have been toast if it wasn't for Fleygur!"

Roger's father reached over to Fleygur and and rubbed his forehead.

Fleygur's eyes were itching from the smoke, so he took the opportunity to have a good rub, smearing the man's shirt with thick black ash.

Across the yard Jones was sitting in the back of an ambulance, clasping an oxygen mask over his mouth and nose. Tears streamed down his face, leaving sooty streaks.

## CHAPTER 33
### Dashed Dreams

The next morning Fleygur and Hercules were standing at the field gate staring at the front door of the house. Roger was late, and Fleygur was expecting his morning carrot. The curtains in the boy's bedroom opened, and Fleygur pricked his ears and bobbed his head in anticipation. Finally, someone was moving. Roger stood in the bedroom window for a long time. Fleygur couldn't sense any feelings from this distance, but something wasn't right. Roger usually flung back the curtains with a big grin on his face, and then, very shortly after he would be flying out of the front door, hopping into his boots, with a breakfast sandwich in his mouth, often with his dad calling, "Don't forget to brush your teeth!"

But today Roger was just standing there, looking down at the horses.

Fleygur bobbed his head again, and whinnied, *where's my carrot?*

After a minute Roger's figure withdrew slowly into the gloom of the bedroom behind him.

Fleygur waited. Hercules got bored and

wandered off to graze, but Fleygur was going nowhere until he had seen his boy again, and got his carrot.

By the time the front door finally opened Fleygur was dozing, resting his hind foot and swishing files away with his tail, but he was on full alert again as Roger came out of the house and across the yard.

Roger's shoulders were slumped, and his face was red. He sighed deeply as he reached Fleygur.

"Oh Fleygur. I wanted to go to the Championships. You were gonna to be brilliant. It's not fair."

Fleygur nosed at Roger's pocket. He'd obviously forgotten about his carrot!

"Sorry, boy," Roger said, fishing in his pocket and offering it up on his flat hand.

*Me too*, nickered Hercules as he came up behind, showing flat-ears to Fleygur as he shouldered him out of the way.

"Oi," said Roger, "no squabbling you two."

As Roger was brushing Fleygur's tail a bike slid to a halt in the gateway to the yard.

"On, no, not her, not now!" Roger muttered to Fleygur as Jess clambered over the gates.

"Oh wow, it's true!" Jess said as she crossed the yard, "Mum said your trailer had been nicked last night."

"Dad's Land Rover too, with all our stuff in.

Haven't even got a saddle now," Roger replied, looking down at his feet and twisting his fingers in Fleygur's mane.

"Scumbags!" announced Jess. "Other places were broken into last night too. Sheds and barns and stuff."

"How do you know that?" Roger absentmindedly scratched under Fleygur's mane.

"Mum's a Police Officer," she said. "She was on duty last night. I heard her telling Jackie about it over breakfast."

"Oh," Roger said, and then went quiet again. Fleygur huffed on the back of his neck, but this didn't even produce a smile.

"Maybe they used your trailer to put it all in. They probably started that fire at Jones's place too…" Jess offered.

"Yeah, they did," said Roger, "and nicked Jones's quad bike. He tried to fight them off, so they torched the barn, with the horses in!"

"Mum said you, and your pony—"

"Horse," Roger sighed

"…you and your *horse* saved Mr Jones from the fire! She said you freed the horses, then dragged him out through the flames!" Jess's eyes were wide, "Mum said you were very brave. A proper hero!" Jess was grinning at Roger. He looked at Jess, a little doubtfully at first.

"Yeah, Fleygur was very brave, and he doesn't

even like Mr Jones," said Roger eventually, smiling a little as he ruffled Fleygur's forelock.

"Mr Jones is pretty scary." Jess agreed. "He set his dogs on me once, when I was biking down his drive. Sorry about your trailer and stuff," she said, "but I've seen you ride that horse with no saddle at all," she continued. "You can still ride. You could come out with me on my bike!"

Roger's eyebrows lifted in surprise, and he didn't seem to know what to say.

"If you want to," Jess said quietly. It was her turn to sound doubtful now.

"It's not just the riding," Roger said. "We were supposed to be going to a lesson today, and next weekend is the Championships. We can't go now. Dad says he will have to save up all over again for a new trailer."

"Maybe you can borrow one?" Jess said brightly.

"We don't know anyone with horse trailers, and we'd have to borrow a car too." Roger said.

"Oh, okay...well...I have to go now. I hope something gets sorted." Jess said, jogging back across the yard. She grabbed her bike and cycled away.

Fleygur followed Roger as he led him over to the schooling area in the field, and stood still as Roger jumped on bareback.

"Well, she was right about one thing," said

Roger, taking up the slack in Fleygur's rope. "We might not be champions this year, but I can still ride!"

Fleygur felt Roger's legs press on his sides, and he took off in tölt around the field. Fleygur knew what was coming next, saddle or no saddle, Roger was practicing their class, the one they would have done at the Championships. Round and round they went, slow tölt, trot, then canter, walk for a breather, and finally fast tölt, Fleygur's mane flying and Roger whooping as they flew past Hercules dozing in the middle of the field.

As they finished the last round Roger slid from Fleygur's back and his brighter mood melted away. Fleygur nuzzled Roger's hands. He seemed so sad. Fleygur stood quietly next to his boy, not really knowing what else to do.

That afternoon Fleygur was snuffling around the edges of the field, looking for tasty herbs to nibble, when he heard a familiar sound. He snapped his head up and looked towards the gate. A large car had pulled into the gateway and Jones was getting out! Feeling the muscles in his belly tighten, Fleygur turned a slow circle, and positioned himself behind Hercules, watching from a safe distance as Roger's father walked across the yard and shook hands with Jones.

Roger came out of the house and looked

across to where Jones and his dad were talking. Worry wrinkles appeared on his face, as he looked between the two men and the horses. Then he crossed the yard and climbed over the field gate to weave his fingers into Fleygur's mane.

*What are they doing?* Fleygur wondered.

Whatever it was, if it involved Jones, it couldn't be good, and Fleygur could tell that Roger's belly was in knots too.

## CHAPTER 34
### The Show Must Go On

After a few minutes Jones opened the boot of his car, lifted out a saddle and hung it on the top bar of the gate. Then he handed Roger's father a large black canvass bag. The two men exchanged a few more words, shook hands and Jones got back into his car and drove away.

Roger's father lifted the saddle off the gate, and balancing it on one arm, he picked up the black bag and walked across the yard to where Roger and Fleygur were waiting.

"Well, well," he said.

"What did he want?" Roger asked, digging his fingers deeper into Fleygur's mane.

Fleygur didn't trust Jones any more than boy did, but surely he couldn't do them any harm now. Not now the boy was his, and he was the boy's.

"This is for you," Roger's father announced, as he put the saddle on the ground in front of him, and handed Roger the bag.

"What?" Roger whispered. He put the bag on the ground and unzipped it. Inside was a smart shiny black bridle, to match the brand new saddle, a bright blue halter with a matching rope, and a black fleecy sweat-rug, with a gold trim, in just Fleygur's size. Fleygur snuffled inside the bag hoping there was something edible, but he was out of luck. Roger pushed Fleygur's nose aside as he looked up at his dad with a bemused expression.

"Apparently," his father explained, "Jones heard about the theft of your stuff and wanted to thank you for saving his life. Quite something I'd say. He's not known for acts of kindness. And that's not all..." A smile spread across Roger's dad's face. "He's coming back on Friday with his trailer. He's going to take us all to the British Championships! What do you think about that?"

Roger had clearly lost the power of speech, because he was just staring at his dad blinking.

"Didn't expect that did you?" said his dad, "I certainly didn't, not after the way he went off without a word after the fire brigade left."

Friday came and so did Jones, sending stones flying as he pulled into the yard and jammed on the brakes. Fleygur snorted and tugged on his rope.

"Easy boy," Roger said, rubbing Fleygur's nose. But Fleygur didn't feel easy, not with Jones nearby, and not with that trailer either. As Jones got out of the car, Fleygur snorted and flung his head up.

Roger and his father packed all their camping gear into Jones' car, while Jones leant on the gate talking into his phone. Then Fleygur's saddle, and the black bag were secured in the front of the trailer. The boy and his father waited in silence until Jones had finished his call.

"Ready?" he said brusquely, and then waving at Fleygur, "Get him in then."

As Roger led him to the trailer, Fleygur trembled, and he hesitated when his front feet touched the bottom of the ramp.

"Come on, Fleygur, if you can walk through fire, you can do this," Roger said, jiggling the rope. Roger seemed confident, and Fleygur trusted him, so he followed Roger into the trailer, and was rewarded with a carrot. When the trailer was closed up and he was alone again he pawed the ground anxiously, but as they pulled from the yard he needed all four feet on the ground to keep his balance.

As they arrived at the Show Ground Fleygur could hear the sounds of humans and horses, busy with their preparations for the competition. The scents of the horses who were soon to be his temporary herd filled his nostrils. He whinnied a hello, and several horses answered his call. Fleygur was glad to get off the trailer and into his little paddock, and even happier to see the red horse he knew in the paddock next to him.

*Hello Red*, he nickered.

The red horse lifted his head, his nose vibrating, *I see you, hello again*, he replied.

It was good to have a friendly neighbour, even if he didn't say much, and Fleygur dropped his head and happily grazed, while Roger and his dad were busy setting up their camp.

The next morning the dew was still heavy on the grass when Roger poked his head through the flaps of the tent. Fleygur nickered to him and pawed the ground, waving his nose in the direction of the other horses, who already had their morning hay ration.

*This boy needs more training, if this was the time he thinks breakfast is served,* he thought.

"Come on Rog, out of the way," said his father from inside the tent. "I need to stretch my back."

Roger crawled out of the tent, and his dad squeezed out behind him, stretching his arms above his head. "That was a cold and uncomfortable night, sleeping on the floor. If you keep up this competing lark we're getting proper camp beds!" he said.

Fleygur stamped the ground again.

Roger was just standing there, looking off into the distance.

His dad gave his hair a friendly ruffle. "Come on, that pony's going to dig his way out if you don't give him some hay soon." He paused. "Rog? What's up? You didn't even tell me off for calling Fleygur a pony!"

Roger turned towards his dad, but still said nothing. His face was pale and Fleygur thought he looked like he was about to be sick.

"I can't do it," Roger said, "All these people... watching...what if I do it wrong?"

"Oh, don't worry so much," his dad said, giving him a hug. "You'll be fine, you've been riding that horse all summer. You just need to get on and do your stuff. Now get him fed and groomed, and don't forget to poo-pick that paddock. I'm going for a shower. I'll pick us up some breakfast. Someone said there were bacon and egg sandwiches on offer from the Club House."

Slinging a towel over his shoulder, and with a tooth brush sticking out of his back pocket, Roger's dad walked off towards a rickety looking shed on the other side of the field.

Roger grabbed an armful of hay and threw it over the fence.

*At last*, Fleygur thought, tucking into the hay as Roger cleaned up the paddock around him.

By the time Roger's father got back with their breakfast sandwiches, Fleygur had finished his hay and Roger had him tied up to the trailer. Fleygur stood quietly, his belly nicely full as

Roger brushed him with one hand, and shoved the bacon and egg sandwich in his mouth with the other, licking the trickle of bright orange yolk that dribbled down the back of his hand. Roger's nervousness faded while they were getting ready, and when he was all tacked up, Roger flipped the reins over Fleygur's head and led him towards the Oval Track.

"Come on," he said to Fleygur, "we're going to watch the class before ours."

Several horses were gathered at the end of a long straight path, next to the Oval Track, waiting their turn. One at a time they raced past where Fleygur and Roger were standing.

"Flying Pace!" said Roger. "I've always wanted to see this."

A beautiful palomino mare, her coat shining gold in the sunlight, sped past them, all four feet off the ground between every stride.

"Wow look at them go!" Roger said, as they whizzed past leaving a trail of dust rising behind them.

"Impressive, isn't it?" said a tall man with black hair, holding a brown horse just behind them. As the golden horse crossed the finish-line two humans who were standing by the trackside raised white flags, and the small crowd burst into applause and cheers. Fleygur jumped at the sound and the brown horse flattened his ears at him for invading his space.

"What's that mean?" Roger asked the man.

"It means the horse stayed in Racing Pace the whole way down the track, so it's a clean run, and her time will count. She's fast. We call her The Queen of Pace. She and that palomino are the current Pace World Champions."

"One day, Fleygur, I will be able to ride like that," said Roger quietly.

*...and I will fly like that too*, thought Fleygur.

Dust blowing off the track drifted across the watching crowd, and into Roger's eyes. He brushed his eyes with his arm, just as his dad walked up behind and squeezed his shoulder. "It's your class next. Just keep breathing, you'll be fine."

As Roger mounted, Fleygur felt the boy's tension building again. He was trembling slightly and there was a funny feeling in Fleygur's mouth, like his bit was vibrating. Roger's shallow breathing made Fleygur feel nervous and he jogged as they entered the warm up area.

"Breathe!" called the boy's father. "You can't ride the whole class holding your breath. You'll pass out!"

## CHAPTER 35
### Little Viking Horse

Roger finally let out a big breath just as their class was called, and Fleygur was glad to be on the move. When he was worried, going somewhere always felt better than staying still.

A voiced boomed from a nearby speaker. "Can we have all riders for the Four Gait Class to the Oval Track please."

As they headed up the path towards the Oval Track Jones's scent wafted into Fleygur's nostrils. He snorted nervously. Jones was standing halfway up the path. Fleygur stopped. Suddenly he was back in Germany, after that boat trip. He remembered the pain in his back, and his mouth. The jabbing and the kicking and the—

"Come on Fleygur," said Roger, squeezing his legs against Fleygur's sides. Roger's voice brought Fleygur's attention back to the present, and he stepped forward, leaving Jones behind him as he strode out onto the track with the other horses. The excitement bubbled up inside him and he whinnied for his friends back in their paddocks.

Roger leaned forward and reached under Fleygur's mane to scratch his neck.

"I'm nervous too, Fleygur, but we can do this."

The bell rang for the start of the class and soon they were slow tölting around the track, Fleygur tuning his steps to the movement of Roger's body. Then Roger leant forward very slightly, and Fleygur launched into his bouncy trot, enjoying the chance to stretch his legs and his neck.

"Good boy!" Roger said, sounding excited. After the trot Fleygur had a chance to rest a while in the walk section of the class, and as Roger slowed his breathing Fleygur relaxed. They'd practiced this a lot at home and Fleygur knew what the boy wanted. He wanted Fleygur to walk forward, but not rush. He wanted him to have long strides, and for his head to be relaxed. Fleygur knew when he'd got it, because it felt good, and he could sense that Roger was smiling. Next Roger urged him into canter. Fleygur bombed around the track, lapping the slower horses.

"It's not a race!" breathed Roger. Fleygur could feel Roger sitting deep in the saddle, trying to slow him up. He slowed his stride, and tucked his back legs underneath him, lifting front legs as high as he could.

"Yes, yes!" Roger whispered.

As they started the fast tölt for the final

section of the class they were close to the horse in front. Fleygur quickly gained ground on him, the thought of catching him spurring him on, but as they got closer the horse in front seemed annoyed that Fleygur was trying to pass him, and started to canter. The horse's rider tried to hold him back and the horse weaved across the track blocking Fleygur's path. Fleygur had to suddenly pull up, nearly losing his balance, and his tölt. They'd never win the class if that happened. Roger was holding his breath again, but Fleygur managed to stay balanced, and as they pulled alongside the other horse, Roger pushed Fleygur on and he streaked away, storming around the corners and racing down the long side to catch, and pass, two more horses. Fleygur loved his fast tölt, and as they come up the final long side of the track he could see Roger's dad cheering with the rest of the crowd.

At the end of the class they all gathered by the exit gate waiting for the scores to be announced. One by one the other horses were called forward to receive their rosettes. In sixth place was the black and white horse who blocked his path. Fifth place, a little brown horse with a girl grinning broadly and waving to her mum. Fourth place, a prancy palomino with a tall thin rider. Third place, the jet-black horse. Then there were just two left. The brown horse with the man with the black hair, and Fleygur and Roger.

"You rode well," said the tall man smiling at Roger. "I think you may have this one."

Roger was holding his breath again and Fleygur, feeling the boy's tension, fidgeted, arching his neck and snorting.

"In second place…," boomed the Speaker's voice "…is Martin on Dynjandi, which means our winner is our new young rider, at their first show, Roger and Fleygur!"

Roger flung himself forward and wrapped his arms around Fleygur's neck.

"We did it!" he whispered.

Fleygur stretched his nose up as Roger scratched his neck. He was breathing hard, but he felt good. He was a proper sports horse now.

"Come forward for your winner's rosette Roger!" the Speaker called, "…and well done. These newcomers show great promise…what a great score for their first time at the British Championships!"

With his red winners rosette flapping on his bridle, Fleygur proudly led the other horses in the victory lap. As they rounded the final corner, he charged up the track in his best fast-tölt, his mane flying wildly behind him. Roger dropped the reins and stood up in the stirrups, punching the air with his fists and whooping!

As they came off the track Roger practically flung himself out of the saddle and into his dad's arms. "We did it!" he said.

"You did indeed," said his father, holding out a piece of carrot for Fleygur. The sweet juices tingled in his hot mouth. Fleygur had barely finished his carrot, and Roger was still talking excitedly about the class, when the voice boomed out from the speakers once again.

"We have a special announcement. The judges have decided to award Roger and Fleygur the Best Partnership Rosette. Nice riding, Roger!"

"Wow!" Roger said, hugging Fleygur for the tenth time.

"...and...," the voice continued, "They received a qualifying mark, and will therefore be invited to represent Great Britain in the International Youth Cup in Denmark next Spring!"

"I told you he was special Dad," said Roger, beaming at Fleygur, "I told you!"

A queue of humans was forming to congratulate them, but Fleygur took a step behind Roger, and snorted nervously as Jones came striding up.

"Well done," said Jones. He spoke in a clipped business like fashion, but for a moment he almost looked like he might smile. "You and that horse seem...well matched."

"Thanks," said Roger, but he didn't seem any more comfortable with Jones nearby than Fleygur did, and looked down at his feet. Roger's father gave the boy a shove in the back and Roger looked up at him, and then at Jones.

"Oh, um, thank you for the saddle and stuff, and for driving us…" he began.

"Yes, well," said Jones abruptly, "I'll drive you and that horse back home, as I said I would, and that's it. I've paid you back now…for what you did. So… that's it!" And he turned on his heels and strode away.

Fleygur was glad Jones didn't have his whip to go tap-tap-tap as he went.

"Strange man that," said Roger's father. "I can't work him out. Once we get home, stay away from him."

"No worries," said Roger, sliding his fingers into Fleygur's mane.

As Roger and his father packed up their camp Philippa arrived, walking up to Fleygur's paddock smiling. "Hello fella," she said, "Didn't you do well!"

Fleygur lipped at her palms. He liked Philippa. She was kind, and she smelt of his first home, and there was the lingering scent of Gydja on Philippa's clothes. Fleygur lightly touched the arm of her jumper with his nose and breathed the scent in deeply.

247

Philippa turned to Roger. "You've done a great job with this horse. I am so happy he has a home with you." She looked at Roger's father. "You should be very proud of your son," she said.

"Oh, I am," he said ruffling Roger's hair, "Very proud."

"It's great news, being selected for the Youth Cup, Roger," Philippa continued."

If you and Fleygur carry on like this, I can see you riding in the World Championships one day!"

As Philippa walked away Roger beamed at his father. "World Championships! Fleygur and I could be there, with the best horses in the world. We can do it, Dad, I know we can!"

Fleygur thought that was enough talking, and it was about time he had another treat. He shoved Roger in the back with his nose. Roger laughed and ruffled Fleygur's forelock.

"That's my boy," Roger said, "My Little Viking Horse."

## THE END

## MORE INFORMATION
### The Origins of Icelandic Horses

Icelandic horses are descended from horses brought by the first settlers of Iceland, between 874AD and 935AD. Those who settled in Iceland came from Norway, Ireland and the Western Isles of Scotland, and native horse breeds from all these places are the ancestors of the modern Icelandic horse.

Once in Iceland the harsh nature shaped the breed over the generations, producing a hardy horse, well adapted to the wild weather and rough terrain. Icelandic horses developed short legs and necks, a long and thick winter coat and an efficient digestive system. They are known for being sure-footed, which is not surprising when you think of the mountains, rivers and lava fields of Iceland.

In June 1783 there was a huge volcanic eruption at Laki in Iceland, which continued to spew into the atmosphere for eight months, and created a haze right across Europe. In Iceland the effects were catastrophic, up to 25% of the human population died, and most of the livestock too. There were around 36,000 horses in Iceland before the eruption, and it is thought that up to 27,000 died due to it. Today's Icelandic horses are descended from the hardy little horses that survived.

Once the horses in Iceland were sufficiently well established to breed it is unlikely that many more horses would have been imported, because of the sea crossing. It is said therefore, that they are pure bred for 1000 years! In 1882 a law was passed forbidding the import of any horses, and this remains in place today, to protect the national herd from diseases. This is the reason that no horse that leaves Iceland can ever return, and also the reason that the Icelandic Horse World Championships are never held in Iceland.

*Horses and humans have shaped each others lives for thousands of years. Can you think of other countries where horses have adapted to the environment, or been bred to do a particular job for humans? How are those horses different from Icelandic horses?*

### Icelandic Horse Names

Icelandic horses are traditionally named in one of a number of ways.

Firstly, they may be named after the Icelandic Sagas, Norse mythology, or Gods and Goddesses. For example Gyðja (Gydja) meaning 'Goddess' or 'fairy,' and Thor and Ódinn, the names of Viking Gods.

Secondly, they are named after the horses colour, character or ability. For example Fleygur, meaning 'the flying one' – obviously named after Little Viking Horse's amazing talents; or Kraftur, meaning 'power,' and Magnus meaning 'great.' Then there is Ragnar, meaning 'strong councillor,' and also the name of a 9th Century Viking.

Lastly, they may be named for animals, birds, or the element of nature. For example Fló, meaning 'flea'; Blossi meaning 'flare,' or Dynjandi meaning 'thundering hooves', and this is also the name of a famous waterfall in Iceland.

And then there are ones that don't meet nicely organised categories, like Flikka – a girl's name. They can also be named for weapons and other artefacts too.

Icelandic Horses have other names too, that show their breeding, like human family or surnames. For example Gyðja frá Kröki (which tells you which farm she is from in Iceland); or Kraftur frá Bringu - a real life world champion horse - there's even a film about him; and Fleygur from Siamber Wen - because he was born in the UK the word 'from' is used, instead of the Icelandic word, frá.

The majority of Icelandic Horse breeders outside Iceland have adopted the same custom for naming horses, and this shows the proper respect for this noble breed. It is not considered proper to name the Icelandic horse in a way that is demeaning.

*If you had an Icelandic horse, what name would you choose in English? Now, find out the Icelandic word for that name, add 'from' or 'frá' and the name of the place you live (your street or town), and you have just named your first Icelandic horse!*

### Icelandic Horse Gaits
### - 'Gait' means the pattern of steps

Like other horses, Icelandic horses can 'walk,' 'trot' and 'canter or gallop.' But Icelandic horses can also tölt. Tölt is a four beat gait, where the feet land on the ground, left hind – left front – right hind – right front, in an even rhythm. Tölt can be performed at all speeds, from a fast walking speed through to canter speed. There is always at least one foot in contact with the ground and this makes the tölt very smooth and comfortable for the rider.

An Icelandic horse that can walk, trot, canter/gallop and tölt is known as a "four gaited horse." Some Icelandic horses prefer trot, others prefer tölt. Most Icelandic horses tölt completely naturally and it is common to see foals tölting after their mothers.

There are also Icelandic horses which are "five gaited." These horses can walk, trot, canter/gallop, tölt and pace. Pace is a two beat gait with a moment of suspension, where all four feet are off the ground, which is why it is sometimes called Flying Pace. The hooves on the same side land almost together. This is a fast gait used for racing, and some Icelandic horses can reach speeds of up to 30mph! Some horses pace slowly (Fleygur's 'jiggy-joggy walk'), which is uncomfortable for the rider and not encouraged.

There is a map, showing the different gaits of the Icelandic horse in the front of the book.

*Did you know that some dogs also 'pace.' If there are not many horses near you, try noticing how dogs are walking and running next time you are out and about. Can you see when their feet are landing on the ground in a 'four-beat,' and when they are 'two-beat.'?*

## MORE INFORMATION

**www.littlevikinghorse.com**
The Icelandic Horse Society of Great Britain
**www.ihsgb.co.uk**
**horsesoficeland.is**
The International Federation of Icelandic Horse
Associations (FEIF)
**www.feif.org**

# ACKNOWLEDGEMENTS

Some years ago, on my commute from Wolverhampton to Birmingham, I was scribbling the early ideas for this story in a notebook. A man sat opposite asked if I was a writer. If I am, I replied, this is the first book I have written. We had a lovely chat, and as he left the train he told me that I could do this, and one day he would be able to say that he had met the author of *Little Viking Horse*. I am sorry that I didn't write his name in my notebook, but if you are reading this...I did it!

I wrote the book, but it would not exist without the support and encouragement of so many, and it would not even have been a glint in my eye without my late husband Roger, and his little Viking horse, Fleygur. It was Fleygur's amazing character - that almost literally spoke to me, and Roger's encouragement that led me to create the Little Viking Horse blog on Facebook, and to start to pen the beginnings of the book. I read my scribblings to Roger after coming home from work each day and he urged me to continue. I am so very sad that Roger did not live to see me finish it, but I am proud that I have, and it is of course dedicated to Roger's memory.

As I write this Fleygur is grazing in the field outside my cottage. A very special horse, and I guess he should be thanked too - I'll take him a nice crunchy carrot when I have finished.

A huge thank you must go to Imogen Cooper and her wonderful team at the Golden Egg Academy. It's hard to sum up in a few words the significance of Imogen's belief in what I was writing, her skilful and tactful editorial feedback, and her on-going support as I made the decision to self-publish. Thanks also to all the Golden Egg writers who have been so encouraging.

I am grateful to all those who have contributed to the final book. Thanks to Emma Finlayson-Palmer for her copy edits and kind comments. The striking cover design by Alison Withey, with photo from fellow Icelandic horse enthusiast, Nicola Guenigualt. Mic Rushen, for her Icelandic Horse Gait Map and illustrations, and Fi Pugh for reading my earlier drafts and making sure that I had not departed too far from reality for the sake of the story. Big thanks to Peter Heathcote, Chair of the Icelandic Horse Society of Great Britain, for his unstinting support and promotion of my project, and FEIF (International Federation of Icelandic Horse Associations) for their support and endorsement.

And finally to my parents, and my brother, sister-in-law and their son - thank you, for everything. I could not have wished for a more supportive and encouraging family.

# ABOUT THE AUTHOR

Catherine lives in Shropshire with two cats, several chickens and her three Icelandic horses, including the real Fleygur and Gydja.

This is Catherine's first novel, but she loves telling stories and has never stopped believing that she can talk to animals - so there may be some more!

CPSIA information can be obtained
at www.ICGtesting.com
Printed in the USA
LVHW020153290921
698984LV00002B/151